"Watching Sabrina work was absolutely impressive," Jack said.

"We should get rid of that old statue out front and put up a monument to Sabrina the mechanic. It would be much more inspiring."

He felt his grin falter as he caught sight of Sabrina's face. The look she was giving him was a few levels short of overwhelming gratitude. Did she think he was being sarcastic? He was teasing about the statue, but he'd meant his original compliment to be taken seriously.

Not knowing what else to say, Jack tried to look as innocent as possible. Those beautiful brown eyes narrowed. He wasn't making it better. He didn't quite understand the emotions that crossed her face, but he wanted to, more than he had wanted anything in a long time. Something about this dark-eyed woman with the soft accent tugged at him.

He cleared his throat and looked away. No matter how intriguing she was, he didn't have the freedom to do anything about it. His life was a complicated mess.

Books by Virginia Carmichael

Love Inspired

Season of Joy
Season of Hope
A Home for Her Family

VIRGINIA CARMICHAEL

was born near the Rocky Mountains, and although she has traveled around the world, the wilds of Colorado run in her veins. A big fan of the wide-open sky and all four seasons, she believes in embracing the small moments of everyday life. A homeschooling mom of six young children who rarely wear shoes, those moments usually involve a lot of noise, a lot of mess or a whole bunch of warm cookies. Virginia holds degrees in linguistics and religious studies from the University of Oregon. She lives with her habanero-eating husband, Crusberto, who is her polar opposite in all things except faith. They've learned to speak in shorthand code and look forward to the day they can actually finish a sentence. In the meantime, Virginia thanks God for the laughter and abundance of hugs that fill her day as she plots her next book.

A Home for Her Family

Virginia Carmichael

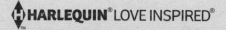

Recycling programs
for this product may
not exist in your area.

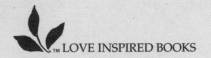 ™ LOVE INSPIRED BOOKS

ISBN-13: 978-0-373-87918-2

A HOME FOR HER FAMILY

Copyright © 2014 by Virginia Muñoz

www.Harlequin.com

Printed in U.S.A.

He said to them, "Go into all the world
and preach the Gospel to all creation."
—*Mark* 16:15

This book is for all those who have loved
and cared for a child who is not their own,
especially foster parents like Mike and Terri Neal.
Your faith, wisdom and tenderness
are powerful weapons in this broken world.

Chapter One

"We've got a crisis of epic proportions." Jack Thorne dodged a flying soccer ball and motioned toward the Downtown Denver Mission's cafeteria kitchen. "One of the big industrial food choppers went on the fritz."

"That's a disaster on a regular day, but right now…" Gavin grimaced and left the rest of the thought unfinished.

"Maybe we should lend a hand."

Jack could see the kitchen staff working frantically, sacks of vegetables and potatoes on every surface. The kids hated to skip a single practice and as the coach, he loved the team's commitment. But with Easter brunch in two days, he wondered if they should just give the kids the evening off. "Not that I have a problem with chopping fifty pounds of potatoes, but there are twenty little kids over there to think about." Gavin nodded toward the players honing their instep kicks, shrieks of laughter echoing around the gym.

"Good shot, William!" Jack clapped for a little blond boy who managed to send the ball somewhere close to his partner. "What's worse, missing practice or missing Easter?"

"The mission will celebrate with or without mashed potatoes. But if you feel that badly, maybe you should make a corporate donation of a large food processor." Gavin grinned, stepping out of the way as a little girl chased a wayward ball. "Just sneak it into the stack of paperwork you sign on a regular basis."

Jack snorted. Being the vice president of Colorado Supplements wasn't quite the way people pictured it. Sure, he was the boss's son and the one poised to take over the state's biggest business, but he didn't have much say on what happened around the place. He was only a figurehead, a desk jockey who was paid to show up and smile. "The paperwork would take months. Easter is in two days. Marisol is losing her mind this very minute."

The mention of his day job made a sour taste rise up in Jack's throat. He'd always known he wasn't cut out for the business world, with its emphasis on the corporate ladder, endless meetings and miles of red tape. And he'd known for even longer that his father planned to turn over the business to his only son. Some called it being groomed from birth, but that was only a miniscule portion of the whole picture. Family expectations, being force-fed his college education and his own years of nodding weakly at every suggestion had helped Jack climb the corporate ladder. Right into the vice president position. The only way out looked like a long fall back to earth and a lot of hurt feelings.

A soccer ball soared alarmingly close to Gavin's head and he ducked, laughing. "I think Grant already called in the mechanic. Let's hope he gets it fixed, or the workers will be pulling an all-nighter."

Jack shook himself out of his depressing thoughts. He waved an arm and jogged toward the lines of kids partnering up near the edge of the gym. Spring was coming, Easter was in a few days and his life was changing. No. Correction: he was making life-changing decisions, taking power back into his own hands, learning to be true to his individual purpose in life.

He drew in a long, deep breath and let it out slowly. God was good, all the time. He knew what he had to do and prayed that his father would forgive him for it.

The gym doors swung open and Lana, the secretary, entered, arms propelling her wheelchair with swift movements. Her purple-tipped crew cut gave the impression of someone with an ingrained toughness who didn't take any guff. That was all true, but Lana's tender patience was the perfect counterpoint to her nononsense attitude. In short, she was the best person to act as gatekeeper to such a large homeless center.

Jack raised a hand in greeting and she smiled back, motioning to the people behind her. A young woman strode through the door, black hair coming loose from its braid. She had dark smudges under her large eyes, as if she hadn't slept well for more nights than she could count. Even though exhaustion was written on her face, her shoulders were straight and her lips set in a firm smile. She held a small dark-haired girl by one hand and in the other she carried a green metal box by the handle. An older child trailed behind, eyes wide as she watched the soccer team. As soon as they were through, Lana went back to the reception area with a wave.

"Uh-oh. Stragglers. I'll go let them know that dinner was over an hour ago." Jack loped away from the group, leaving Gavin to supervise. Maybe Marisol had something left over for these three. He sure hoped so. The mom looked as if she needed a place to sit down and rest for a minute. Or a day or two.

As he got closer, the woman met his gaze, a direct question in her dark eyes. But they ended up speaking at the same moment.

"Can I help you?"

"Can I help y—?" Jack broke off at the last word, laughing. Not sure why he'd need help at his own soccer practice, but he liked her answering smile.

She was at least half a foot shorter than he was and titled her head up as she stepped closer. "I'm sorry to interrupt your practice. Go ahead. We'll keep out of your way." She had a soft accent, her vowels ringing pure and clear.

"Dinner was over a while ago. I think the head cook, Marisol, might have something left. I can go see, if you and your girls want to wait here." He glanced at the little kids, noting both had the same heart-shaped face and thickly lashed dark eyes as their mom. They peered back shyly, as if he was the strangest part of their day by far. The younger one met his gaze and dropped her head, staring down at her scuffed sneakers. Her little chin tucked into her chest, as if she was trying to disappear. The hem of her pink T-shirt was unraveling and her pants were threadbare at the knees.

The woman's brows arched up. "Thank you, we've had dinner. Grant called me to fix the kitchen equipment." She lowered the green case to the ground. The faint sound of metal tools echoed back. "But I don't want the girls in the kitchen while I work. It's not safe."

She glanced at the group of kids practicing long passes. "Is it possible they could stay out here and watch?"

Jack struggled to catch up, feeling as though he'd assumed too much, although he was certain female mechanics were few and far between. "Sure. I can let them have some balls to kick around here at the end." He paused. "I'd let them join the group for tonight, but all the parents have to sign waivers before their kids can play."

She held out her hand, corners of her mouth tilted up. "Thank you. I'm Sabrina Martinez. This is Kassandra and Gabriella."

Jack took her hand and nodded, thinking he had never heard such beautiful names said in quite that way. Soft, musical, like a few notes of a song.

"And you are?" she prompted him, dark eyes crinkling at the corners. Her hand was warm and soft, not the sort of hand he'd imagine for a mechanic.

He cleared his throat. All that time sitting in a boardroom with sixty-year-old men and he was losing his touch. "Jack Thorne."

"Can we, *Tía?* Please?" The older girl tugged on her aunt's hand. "We'll be really good."

In response, the woman flashed a smile that made Jack blink. "Best behavior, remember."

The two nodded, dark ponytails jumping in unison, and exchanged gleeful looks.

"I'll head on in, and thanks again." She adjusted her backpack and picked up the green box. He couldn't imagine how much it weighed, but she lifted it easily.

"No problem." His voice sounded odd to his own

ears. The slightest whiff of cinnamon followed her as she brushed past.

Gavin's voice reminded Jack he had a team to coach. "Looks like we've got visitors." It wasn't a question, but a friendly statement, and the girls responded with identical grins.

"This is Kassandra and Gabriella." He tried to say it just like Sabrina had, but it came out sounding as if he was a stuffy Italian duke in need of a kingdom. "Their mom is working on the food chopper so they'll just hang out near the end zone for a while."

"She's our aunt," Gabriella volunteered. "And you can call me Gabby."

"I'm Kassey," whispered the younger one.

Gavin went down on one knee and shook each small hand. "Well, *princesas,* find a ball and enjoy yourselves. We'll be over there."

The two girls giggled simultaneously and trotted off to retrieve a soccer ball.

"Impressive." Jack shot Gavin a look. *"Princesas?* Please tell me that's not the only word you know in Spanish."

As they turned back to the kids practicing drills, Gavin said, "I've been taking classes for a few weeks. And every girl wants to be a princess, right? It doesn't hurt to throw that in during the conversation."

"I'll make a note. As always, I'm running to catch up with the wonderful Gavin Sawyer. If you weren't my favorite brother-in-law, you would really be getting on my nerves."

"I'm your only brother-in-law." Gavin scooped up a stack of orange cones and handed them to Jack. "And I'm only trying to catch up to that pretty twin sister of yours. She's always cooking up some new plan to save the world." Gavin paused, thinking. "No, that's not right. She's never trying to save the whole world. Just her little corner, one person at a time." His smile said more than his words could, about how Evie inspired him, how she had taught him to hope.

Jack wanted to roll his eyes at the expression on Gavin's face, but part of him wished he knew how it felt to be so deeply in love. He'd always thought he'd find the right girl, settle down, have a few kids, nothing complicated about it. Now all those steps would have to wait awhile. He was on the verge of leaving a high-paying position with a guaranteed future for financial uncertainty. No woman would see him as a good candidate for marriage if he walked away from a life of security. He had his reasons, but they were hard to explain. Something about God's will for his life and being true to his calling. Definitely not ideas he could toss around on a first date.

He laid out the orange cones in a line around the cafeteria and tried to shrug off the suspicion he had wasted the best years of his life as a corporate flunky. He'd tried to make the job work, tried to get involved in other levels besides meeting and greeting VIP visitors to Colorado Supplements. But last week's meeting with Bob Barrows had clinched his decision. The way Barrows had mocked him for wanting to see the production statistics still rang in his head. He was just the boss's kid and that would never change. Not there anyway.

It was time for new chapters. He had his savings, a long list of clients built up and an excellent reputation as one of the best snowboarders in Denver.

He was going to focus on disentangling himself from

the family company and salvaging his relationship with
his father. Sabrina's teasing expression flickered into
his mind. Beautiful, accented women wielding tools
were not on the radar, unfortunately. He had plenty of
work to do on his own life without making it any more
complicated.

"Sabrina, *mija!*" Marisol grabbed her in an enormous
hug that squeezed the air out of her. Sabrina suspected
the enthusiastic greeting was less for her personally than
for her toolbox, but she returned it with equal fervor. It
was the nicest thing that had happened to her all day and
she savored the warmth of her embrace for a moment.

"Show me the equipment and I'll get started." She
glanced around at the hurrying kitchen staff. Two days
before Easter was pretty bad timing. *Dios, ayude me.*
The mission needs this machine to work.

Marisol motioned her to the Hobart chopper and
hurried away, calling over her shoulder, "Thank you!"
Lines of kitchen staff stood side by side at the long steel
tables, chopping vegetables.

Sabrina stood in front of the old Hobart and tried
not to groan. They had met before and it hadn't been a
pleasant experience. Sure, it could process six hundred
pounds of potatoes an hour, but it was still a cranky old
piece of equipment. The blades were sharp and most
of the gears were new, but the motor was barely clank-
ing along.

She sighed and set her toolbox on the ground. Running from job to job all that day, she had just sunk into
her couch and whispered a prayer of thanksgiving when
the phone rang. She'd hustled the girls out of their bath
and minutes later been out the door again, Kassey and

Gabby in tow. Her mothering skills left a lot to be desired. The poor kids should be in bed, not running all over town.

Straightening up, she brushed back her hair. No, that was no way to think. Her nieces were loved and safe and fed. If everything went well, she'd be their permanent legal guardian within months. She did the best she could and God always filled in the gaps. Self-pity would have to wait for another day.

Soft voices interrupted her thoughts. Marisol had her arm around a young girl, speaking in Spanish to her in soothing tones. She couldn't have been more than twenty, but looked frail and small. Her face was pinched, her shoulders hunched and the kitchen apron swamped her tiny frame. Large dark eyes darted back and forth, as if searching for danger.

"You're okay here, Jimena. No one will hurt you. It is loud, but you are safe."

Sabrina focused on her toolbox and tried not to listen. But the expression on the young girl's face seemed close to panic. Why would anyone be scared of working in the kitchen? Maybe the equipment made her nervous. She could understand some people, especially those new to the large machines, not feeling comfortable around the loud motors.

"I can leave anytime? I can go?" Jimena's voice trembled at every word.

"Of course. Do you want to go back to your room?"

Sabrina peeked up to see Marisol ushering the girl back toward the kitchen entryway.

Jimena stopped, taking deep breaths, dark eyes still wide with fear but not as panicked. "I—I would like to try to work here. Just for a little while."

"Come stand by me. We will work together. And give yourself time. You have been through a very bad experience." Marisol slipped her arm around the girl's shoulder. "No one blames you, Jimena. You went for a job. Those men were criminals and they will be caught."

The two walked slowly back to the gleaming metal table. Jimena stayed close to Marisol, choosing a knife and beginning to work.

Sabrina stared unseeing at the concrete floor. Just when she thought her life was difficult, she heard of something worse. Much worse. She couldn't even imagine what might have happened to that girl, but she could guess. Stories swirled about young people, especially girls, being lured to job sites and then never being allowed to leave. Months of slave labor was the very least of what happened, and even that was enough to scar a person deeply.

She swallowed. It happened, and more often than anyone thought. A lack of education and family meant desperation. Starvation. Utter poverty. Images of her nieces, laughing and running toward the soccer ball, made her throat constrict. *Please, God. Help me keep them from all harm. Help us stay together. Help the judge see that I'm capable of caring for them.*

Shrugging off her backpack, she pulled out her coveralls and slipped them on. It was warm in the kitchen, but she never went without her hard hat and safety goggles, even if it meant she was going to be sporting crazy hair and sweaty lines on her face. She glanced at her hands and saw the grease under her nails. Jack had almost swallowed his tongue when she'd shaken his hand. She could see why. A man like Jack was probably surrounded by polished women who got professional hair-cuts and manicures.

She felt her lips tug up at the thought of what Maya would do at the sight of Jack. Maya, who lived upstairs, was nineteen and officially boy crazy. She would have at least gotten a phone number. The man was obviously athletic, impressively muscled, attired in expensive athletic gear—those things warranted that first glance. Then there was the classically handsome face and shockingly blue eyes, and a matching set of dimples upped the swoon factor. A man like that could have any woman he wanted.

But enough of the daydreaming. She needed to focus or they'd be here all night.

She laid out her small tools and started to remove the front of the food processor. The hinged hood would have to be secured so she could get underneath. Sabrina turned to her toolbox, shaking her head.

"What? It can't be fixed? We will cancel Easter?" Marisol's worried voice cut through her thoughts.

"No, sorry, just thinking." She reached out and squeezed the woman's shoulder. "I need a prop for the hood."

Marisol blinked, not understanding.

Sabrina switched to Spanish while peering around the kitchen for something the right height. There had been a metal prop attached to the inside of the Hobart once upon a time, but it had long ago broken off and been discarded. Could she use a chair? No, the legs would be in her way. Frustration coursed through her. She had a small jack that expanded to four feet and supported a hundred pounds, just for machines like the old Hobart, but she'd left it at home.

Marisol lifted a finger in the just-a-minute gesture. "Wait here."

Sabrina nodded. Not much choice. She could still loosen the parts on the bottom while Marisol went to fetch a small stool or ladder. The machine was clogged with hours-old potato pieces and she scooped the remains to the side, the dank smell clinging to her snug-fitting work gloves. She didn't mind engine grease, but rotten-vegetable wasn't high on her list of wearable perfumes.

The enormous kitchen echoed with the steady sound of knives hitting chopping blocks and the dishwasher running in the corner. She felt the rhythm of the place, as comforting as a heartbeat, and relaxed into the work. Her small power drill made a quick job of the screws and in a few minutes the machine stood exposed. Sabrina sat back on her heels and wiped the sweat from her face with one arm.

"Nice hat."

She startled backward at the deep voice and landed directly on her bottom. Her face flamed as she scrambled back to her feet. The good-looking soccer coach was feet away, perfectly at home in the mission kitchen.

Touching the back of her hard hat, she remembered Gabby's little gift. She'd earned it at school and Sabrina couldn't bear to get angry over the fact it had ended up on her work uniform. It was an act of little-girl generosity, because Gabby had been sure her aunt wanted a big sparkly pink star of her very own. "Do you need something?"

He laughed, bright eyes locked on her face. "You keep asking me that."

"Are the girls okay?"

"Everybody's fine." He moved closer to the Hobart. "Marisol said you needed help."

Of course. The way this day was going, she should have guessed that Marisol wouldn't bring a ladder or a prop. She would bring a man, and one who spoke in a deep, chocolaty baritone that made Sabrina wish she wasn't wearing coveralls and coated in potato peels. She blew out a sigh and jerked her shoulder toward the metal sheet that was the front of the chopper.

"I need to get into the engine, but there's nothing to hold up the cover." Searching for a tool spared her from having to make eye contact and seeing the look on his face.

"Sure." He stood close to the cover, one hand on the edge. "There's no way to lock the hinge?"

"No. I usually have a prop, but I forgot it at home." The idea of him hovering as she worked made her palms sweat. "It's up right now, but with all the vibration of the machinery, it could fall while I'm working. I don't want my nose squashed into the gears if I can help it."

"I'll be the spotter." He set his feet apart, seeming comfortable enough.

"Spotter?"

"It's a sports term. You're the athlete and I'm the person who stands nearby to catch you if you fall." He was smiling that slow smile that started at the corners of his mouth and worked toward his eyes.

Sabrina nodded and ducked under the hood, swallowing back a sudden wave of emotion. It had been a very long time since anyone had been there to catch her. Even when her parents were alive, she had been the one responsible for interpreting for them, for talking to bosses and apartment managers. After her mother died, her dad's drinking meant she was head of the household at sixteen. It was impossible to keep her little sister under control. By the time Rosa was twenty, she'd had two babies. Another year and she'd been gone, off to live with some guy she met on the internet, a guy who didn't want the responsibility of kids.

Turning a wrench with a quick twist of her wrist, Sabrina tried to focus on the job at hand. Responsibility was her middle name. All work and no play was her motto. It was nice to think of having a partner, to not be the only one in charge, but in the end it was all up to her. Better to face that fact and not be disappointed. Plus, when fighting for custody, the court looked more kindly on a woman who was focused on the kids and not her social life.

"Do you carry all your tools in your trunk?" His voice came from somewhere right above her head.

"My trunk?" It was easier to talk this way, as if she was talking to the grumpy Hobart.

"Of your car."

"Oh." She dropped a few bolts into the tin near her foot. "I don't have a car. We took the bus."

There was a pause. Sabrina stared at the shiny blades of the peeler. She didn't like taking the bus with two little girls at this hour of the night, but a job was a job, especially since the rent just went up. Again. There were only so many hours in the day. Soon it wouldn't matter how much she worked—they would have to move to a smaller apartment in a tougher neighborhood.

"My nieces are pretty good about staying out of the tools, but thanks again for letting them play in the gym. When I was taking night classes, they sat in the hallway, right outside the open doorway of the classroom.

It was tough, even with picture books and crafts. A few professors would let them sit in the back of the room, but they still had to be quiet."

"Not a problem. They're having a great time. In fact, they're better than most of the regular team. Does their mom work at night?"

She reached for a rag to wipe off more potato sludge and said, "They live with me." The whole story was too complicated for the moment. She hoped he understood that. The story of her childhood, her dad's drinking and her sister's wild life wasn't something she shared with anybody outside of a court. Even then, it was humiliating to own the disaster of her family life and the poverty of her past. She needed to prove to the court she was the best one to take care of the girls. If they ended up in foster care, her heart would break.

"Interesting. I've never met a—"

With a loud clank, the tool slipped from her hand and rolled a few feet away. Sabrina closed her eyes, wishing she could click her heels and the chopper would be fixed. He'd never met a what? A single mother? A fractured family?

He stuck out one foot, not leaving his post by the heavy raised cover, and nudged the wrench back in her direction as if it was a soccer ball. "I've never met a professional juggler."

She snorted. So he was funny as well as athletic and gorgeous. "Just a mediocre one, actually."

"That's the thing about juggling. It's really impressive to the person watching."

She couldn't help smiling as the final gear came loose. Even though she usually worked in silence, it felt good to talk to someone older than Kassey. The kitchen sounds were soothing now, less frantic. She wondered if Marisol had sent some of the staff home, but she didn't turn around to check. The clock was ticking.

"How did you decide to become a mechanic?"

Another swipe of the rag and the last half-peeled potato came out of the chopper. "I took classes."

Jack laughed, a sound rich and deep. She felt it from the base of her skull all the way down her spine. "Before that. Did you know it was your calling?"

She shook out the rag and sat back for a second, meeting his gaze. "My calling?"

He nodded, his expression completely serious. "Your purpose in life, if you want to call it that."

She dropped her gaze to the toolbox and kept her face straight as she searched for the locking pliers.

"You want to say something, but you're too polite."

Startled, she let out the laugh she'd been hiding. "True."

"Go ahead, be honest. I can take it." And for all his obvious strength, she wondered if he could. It took a lot more than muscles to handle honesty; it took maturity. He looked about her age, maybe a few years closer to thirty.

Sabrina drew in a breath and hoped she was being honest but not rude. Life was too short to be mean. "Finding your purpose in life sounds like something rich people worry about when they have a lot of options."

His face didn't change, but his gaze sharpened, as if he was seeing her for the first time. "And you don't have options."

"Not many. Not like that." She ducked back under the hood and hoped that was the end of the conversation.

She felt raw, as if he had stripped back layers of accumulated worry and anxiety. The question of purpose, of calling, was something she used to understand. But that was before Rosa had walked away and left her the mother to two little girls.

"You must have a few."

"Sure," she said, feeling a bead of sweat roll down the back of her neck as she worked at an old bolt. "I can fail or I can work harder."

"Like the rest of us, then." He wasn't letting the question go and frustration flared inside her, just for a moment. Who was he to ask questions that were already answered? Who really cared why she was a mechanic?

She grabbed a can of industrial solvent and sprayed the inside of the stubborn part. The fumes were a reminder of the dirty, complicated job she did on a daily basis. She had to admit, she hadn't chosen to be a mechanic because it seemed like fun.

Twisting the sharp steel disks deep in the machine, Sabrina felt his silence like a steady presence. It was the first time in years that anyone had really cared why she did what she did, let alone asked. She was the responsible one, the girl everyone could count on, the one who never dropped a ball.

Crawling out from under the hood, she stood with the wrench in one hand and a rusty bolt in the other. "I decided to be a mechanic because I love working with metal." She waited for his look of confusion, for those dark brows to jerk up in surprise, for a deep laugh at the concept of loving something most people never even noticed.

"What kind of metal?" Jack's expression was pure curiosity, nothing more.

"Brass, iron, aluminum. I used to love copper, but that was in my flashy phase."

He was staring at her, eyes filled with something she couldn't quite define. She ducked back under the hood. "I think once I get the inside put back together, it's going to work. Seemed to be jammed." She sure hoped it was a jam and not an engine failure. Marisol was going to have a breakdown if Easter brunch was postponed.

For once there was silence from Jack. She'd thought she wanted the peace, didn't need the distraction, but she kept listening for the sound of his voice. His presence was distracting and comforting at the same time, and as her hands replaced part after part, she couldn't help wondering what it would be like to get to know him better, sometime when she wasn't wearing coveralls and a hard hat. He probably had a girlfriend.

Shaking the thoughts from her head, Sabrina tried to focus on the stubborn old machine in front of her. She'd really been working too hard. Her emotions were a mess. All it took was one handsome guy paying her a bit of attention and care, and suddenly she was planning their next date. And she didn't have the leisure to plan anything more than how to get custody of the girls. That was her sole aim and nothing was going to shake her focus.

It was imperative she show the courts she was steady, reliable and responsible. As soon as she was given custody, they'd find a cheaper place to live. They loved the apartment, true, but she couldn't keep working around the clock like this. And she couldn't move now or she might look unstable.

If it weren't for Rosa and that no-good boyfriend…

A flash of anger swept through her and she let out a deep breath, willing herself to focus on forgiveness.

Out of the corner of her eye, she could see Jack standing there. He was so quiet. She wondered what he was thinking and then was irritated at herself for wondering. It didn't matter what this guy thought of her. The only thing she could focus on right now was keeping the girls in the only family they'd known.

If they could just hang on a little longer, she would be their legal guardian and they could find another place. As it was, she was barely paying the bills. They were getting poorer by the month and something had to give. But it wasn't going to be their little family; she would make sure of that.

Jack gripped the hood of the old chopper and stared into space. He had asked what he'd thought was a simple question about her life choices, but her answer hadn't been what he'd expected. He'd assumed so much without realizing it. It had never been clearer to him that he was coasting along in life, hardly working for the things that he needed. Every door was open to him, but he was passing time in his father's company and playing businessman. The young woman crouched by his feet had just knocked the breath out of him and didn't even notice. He struggled to slow his pounding heart. He had been so sure that he wasn't meant to work at the family company, and now, after one conversation in a noisy kitchen, he was seeing it from a whole new angle. He had stayed because of his dad's heart attack, but Jack was easing his way out of the business just as his dad was getting better. But now he wondered, who was he to quit a well-paying job because he wasn't particularly *happy?* So what if Bob from packaging and distributions had made him feel powerless?

The pettiness of it all made him sick to his stomach. This beautiful girl did what she could and didn't complain about it, even as she scooped out rotting potato parts from old machines. Why? Because she was being a mother to two little girls who needed her. The utter selflessness of her story made him want to hang his head. He had wasted months dithering over whether to start a snowboarding company on Wolf Mountain, while families like hers were fighting to survive.

"Go ahead and lower the hood." Sabrina scooted out from under the machine, grabbing the power cord. "I want to see if this crusty old thing will run. Say a prayer."

Lowering the hood, he stepped back and watched her flip the switch. The engine roared to life and the kitchen erupted into cheers. Marisol flew at Sabrina, chattering in warp-speed Spanish, tears of happiness making tracks on her deeply lined brown cheeks. He couldn't help but grin at the expression on Sabrina's face. Half amusement, half relief.

She flipped the machine off and found her drill, making quick work of replacing the bolts. She stood up and looked over at him. "Thanks for your help. Marisol says she's going to make you tamales."

"Well, if I'd known there was a reward, I would have volunteered right away." He pasted on a bright smile, hoping she couldn't see how rattled he was by their conversation. As it was, she just laughed and brushed off the knees of her coveralls.

"Would you let the girls know we've got to get going?

I'll just clean up here and be right out." She took off the hard hat and started gathering her tools.

"Will do." He turned to the gym, feeling as if his legs were made of lead. In all his prayers over God's purpose for his life, as he'd struggled over how to find happiness, he had never once considered that he should just work harder at his job.

A ten-minute conversation with a woman in coveralls had given him a dose of reality. He glanced back, watching her carefully replace her tools in the green metal box. With her fragile features and dark hair pulled back in a loose ponytail, she looked like any other young woman, but the resolute set of her jaw belied the strength inside. She did what she had to do.

Who was he to walk away from that much money when other people were struggling? *Finding your purpose sounds like something rich people worry about when they have a lot of options.* Her words echoed around his head, making his worry seem selfish and small.

Jack watched Kassey and Gabby kick the soccer ball back and forth. Joyous and carefree, they were happy because of Sabrina. His father was happy he worked at the family company. Maybe it didn't really matter how useful he was. Maybe his purpose wasn't tied to his occupation. Maybe it was a state of being. Generosity, sacrifice and hard work made people happy, not the job.

He let out a deep breath and straightened his shoulders. It would be months before his dad was well enough to put in a full day as head of the company. He would take it one day at a time. Maybe Sabrina's way was better and putting his own happiness a little farther down the list of priorities would give him peace. He didn't have anything to lose. Anything had to be better than pretending to love life as the company puppet.

"*Tía* Sabrina, we want to join the team!" Kassey ran across the gym floor with her arms open wide, glossy black hair falling out of her pigtails. Her grin was so wide Sabrina could see all her little teeth. She wrapped herself around Sabrina's waist and beamed up with the perfect confidence of a child.

"We do, we do!" Gabby added her voice to the pleading, tiny hands pulling on Sabrina's pant leg.

"I think the soccer team is for the mission children." She felt the familiar sting of having to say no and wished for once, just once, it could be different. She rubbed a hand over Kassey's hair, feeling the strands flow through her fingers like water.

Jack walked toward them, a soccer ball under one arm. The rest of the children were being met by their parents and excited voices filled the echoing space. "Actually, any children can join. We started our own team here because the residents have trouble getting to the city league practices. And we do have a few openings."

Setting down her toolbox on the polished gym floor, she glanced up into those bright blue eyes and searched for words. Any words. She wanted to nod and agree, but she couldn't. She had to explain that there was no way she afford sports equipment on top of school supplies, no way she could bring the girls to practice at the mission every day while taking evening jobs, and absolutely no way she could handle one more task in her life. She just couldn't.

He went on, his deep voice carrying easily through the noise around them. "We only have practice twice a week, Thursday and Friday. All the equipment is paid for through a special grant organized by one of the local churches."

"Please?" Kassey managed to make the word into several syllables while her voice rose two octaves.

"I don't know, sweetie. We just have so much going on…" Her voice trailed off at the look on her niece's face. Disappointment, then a brave attempt to blink back tears.

"Okay." Kassey nodded and took Gabby's hand. They stood quietly, waiting to go home.

Sabrina sighed. They had sacrificed so much, had lost everything once before. If they had whined and fussed, it would be easier to say no. But that quiet strength tugged at her heart. She turned to Jack, narrowing her eyes. "Tell me the truth. What kind of time commitment is this? And is it really no charge? The equipment is free, but are there team fees? Game fees? Travel fees?"

"Two practices a week. Games on Saturday afternoon at the inside field on Stanton. Everything free." He didn't glance at the girls or encourage them at all, and she was thankful for that. He was giving her space to consider, letting her make the decision without any pressure.

"So, they need to try out? What if one gets in but not the other?" She crossed her arms. Stanton Avenue wasn't far from their apartment. She could walk them down there. No fees and maybe the schedule would work, but these two girls had feelings she needed to consider, too.

He leaned close, dropping his voice. She caught the light scent of soap and masculinity. "We don't really have tryouts. The kids come and we sign them up. Everybody learns together." He stood back and the corners of his lips turned up, as if they were sharing a secret.

Heat crept up her neck and she dropped her gaze to Kassey's hopeful eyes. This was about the girls, not the coach, although her brain was gibbering something about how seeing Jack two times a week could be very interesting. Maybe she wouldn't even stink of rotten potato peel next time. "Homework will always have to be done first. And you have to be team players. And help each other."

They both let out tiny shrieks of happiness. "We will, we promise!" Matching pairs of dark eyes shone with joy and Sabrina savored the feeling of being the hero for once. She was always the one who had to say no. But not today.

"Thank you." The words came out huskier than she'd intended. Her throat felt tight and she swallowed away the sudden emotion. "It's been a long time since they've gotten to do something really fun."

"No problem." He laid a hand on Kassey's shoulder, face serious. "Next practice is Thursday. You two are saving the team. We were short a few players and now we'll have enough alternates that no one will get too tired out during the game." He was speaking to them as if they were newly acquired star players.

Their expression of wide-eyed glee made her breath catch. There were caring teachers at school and sweet Mrs. Guzman from upstairs. But there was a hole in their lives where a mom and dad should be. She was determined to keep them together as a family, but she knew what she gave them wasn't always enough. She did her best to fill a mom's shoes, but this kind of validation, from someone like Jack, meant more than she'd realized.

Chapter Two

The shrill sound of a whistle cut through her thoughts. "Hey, I'll be back." Jack jogged off to the other side of the gym and started to round up the straggling kids into the group. Sabrina watched his easy stride, the generous smile and wondered what it was about him that made her think he was a little restless. As if there was too much energy for one body, or he had other plans for the rest of the evening.

Actually, he probably did. A guy like that wouldn't be unattached. She shrugged off the curiosity and tried to focus on the excited chatter from her nieces.

"We'll work really hard," Gabby said, lapsing into Spanish as soon as Jack left.

"We promise." Kassey was so earnest that Sabrina almost laughed. Usually she preferred they speak Spanish only at home, but she didn't correct them. It made her smile just to see how thrilled they were at the idea of running drills and practicing kicks. They knew the custody hearing was coming up in two months and they were as nervous as she was. Nervous and worried and unsure of what the future held. This would give them something to do besides worry.

"I know you will. I have no doubt." She gathered them to her, one on each side. "You always make me proud." Leaning down to kiss one small head, then another, she knew that whether or not they scored a single goal, being on the team would be a gift to their self-esteem. *Lord, as always, You are full of surprises.*

Sabrina glanced back toward Jack, watching him chat easily with the parents who'd arrived to collect their kids. He seemed to be one of those people who made friends with everyone, anywhere, anytime. Even knowing that, she couldn't shake the memory of how it felt to talk with him. She felt heard, for the first time in a long time. Maybe that's why she'd talked about how she loved metal and machinery. It certainly wasn't something she shared every day. Or at all, really. Of course, no one had ever asked her why she wasn't a secretary or a preschool teacher, something more feminine. She'd heard plenty of comments in the past two years. Some people thought it was cute, some people thought it was weird and a lot of people thought it was a man's job. But no one had ever asked her why.

Gabby was speed talking her way through a wish list of soccer gear and Sabrina nodded, not really listening. Jack seemed so full of energy, so much more alive than anyone around him. What was it about him that made her want to stop and take a deep breath, to shrug off her massive schedule for just one moment and do something fun?

He met her gaze across the gym and she turned away, embarrassed to be caught staring. Whatever the reason she'd shared her past, it was a sure sign that she needed to get out more. One short conversation and she was overthinking her life. It didn't matter why she did the job she did and it certainly didn't matter what he thought about her.

She had one goal, and that was to get legal custody of the girls. To do that, she needed to keep them afloat, pay the rent on time and look like a responsible parent. Maybe when it was all over she could think about her own needs. For now, she just had to keep her head down and do what needed to be done, and that included avoiding Mr. Deep Thoughts. As cute as he was, she wasn't going to be having another heart-to-heart with Jack Thorne again anytime soon.

"Gavin will be over in a minute to talk to you. He's the other coach and has the schedule for next week," Jack said. He must have startled Sabrina, because she jumped at the sound of his voice. "And some waivers to sign. You're their legal guardian?"

"Temporary. There's a hearing soon and we're hoping it will be settled by the time summer starts. They want to give my sister the chance to contest the motion. Every time they set a date, Rosa says she's coming back for the hearing, but then she'll ask to postpone it. This is the last time she can ask to retain her rights, and I don't think she'll show up." Her face was stoic but there was an old sadness in her eyes. One hand smoothed Gabby's dark hair in an absentminded motion.

He wanted to say something but wasn't sure what. *Congratulations* didn't seem right.

"*Tía,* you should help. You love soccer." Gabby tugged on her aunt's hand.

"Yes, you should," Kassey chimed in. "Coach Jack, she played on a soccer team, too."

"Did you? We need another coach here." Jack grabbed at that fact like a drowning man. They could talk soccer. That was a safe subject.

"Only in high school. It wasn't anything."

"On a team?" Gavin returned from the supply closet. "We really do need someone, especially someone who can speak Spanish. Some of the newer residents have trouble following the directions and Jack's Spanish isn't up to speed."

Jack resisted giving Gavin a casual punch on the arm. The man knew a few words and thought he was fluent.

Sabrina laughed and the sound stopped Jack in his tracks. She was so beautiful. He'd already known that, but when she laughed, it was as if a light had been turned on inside and she shone for the world to see.

"I suppose if you need a token Spanish speaker, I could lend a hand. I'll be here anyway since we take the bus back and forth."

"So?" Gavin's voice held laughter.

"So, what?" Jack turned, frowning.

"I asked you what you thought. Should we nominate Sabrina for coach status?" Gavin was chuckling now, not even bothering to hide his amusement. "Looks like we lost you somewhere along in this conversation."

Sabrina's brows drew down. She said, "You know, it's really okay. If you don't think it's a good idea—"

"No, I think it's a great idea."

"Then it's settled. Welcome, Coach Sabrina," Gavin said.

She grinned. "Thanks."

"Jack." He turned his head and saw Jose winding his way through the gym. The stocky man's dark skin couldn't hide the tattoos visible from biceps to wrist, but his red polo was neatly pressed. Grant had all the mission staff wear a uniform, mostly for simplicity, but it also was a sign to the residents of who was an official staff member. "Are you teaching snowboarding classes this spring? My nephew wants to learn."

"Not right now. Probably not until October." It killed Jack to say it, but snowboarding was on hold. Actually, his entire plan of launching a business of snowboarding clinics up on the mountain was in limbo.

Jack glanced at Sabrina and saw her eyes flick to Jose's tattoos. He could understand her wariness, especially if she knew the meanings behind the markings. Jose had turned his life around, but his body still bore the marks of a life on the streets. "Jose, this is Sabrina Martinez."

He held out a hand with a wide smile. "I'm the intake specialist. Mostly paperwork. Very boring."

"Oh," she said, and then recovered quickly. Jack could tell she was surprised that Jose was staff and not a resident. "Nice to meet you."

Jose turned back to Jack. "Well, if you change your mind, I've got a ten-year-old who's nagging me to death for lessons." He started for the cafeteria door.

"If I could save you from that, I would," Jack answered a little wistfully. He would love to be spending all his time up on the mountain instead of behind a desk.

"Look, there's the director." Jack waved an arm and called, "Grant, would you like to meet our newest team members?"

The dark-haired director carried his little boy in his

arms, his red tie wrapped firmly in the toddler's fist. "Sabrina, I should have warned you about Jack and his ability to draw people into the team." His voice was layered with good humor. "And these two young ladies seem to be the very players we needed. God sent you to us just in time."

Kassey and Gabby smiled shyly. Jack caught Sabrina's gaze and he winked. Between Gavin's *princesa* comment and Grant's directorial blessing, these two were going to pop with happiness. He loved this nonpaying job more than anything he'd ever done as a VP. In a world that seemed cold and ugly, all of this attention was just what the girls needed.

"Sabrina, tell me you fixed the old Hobart. I'm afraid to go in there. Marisol might eat me alive, so I'm bringing Gabriel for protection," Grant said.

"Abuelita!" The little baby crowed the word and pointed to the kitchen. His blue eyes were fixed on the entrance as if Marisol would exit at any moment.

"See? He knows where he can find her. In a moment, buddy." Grant's smile faded and his heavy brows drew down. "Either the machine was too broken to fix or it was a simple cleanup job. Please tell me it was the latter."

"I took off the front panel and cleaned out the pieces. All the slicers looked fine, but there was half a potato jammed into the main hopper. All it needed was a little industrial solvent, a bit of degreaser and—" she glanced at Jack "—a spotter. Seems to be running okay now."

Relief filled Grant's eyes. "Wonderful. You're worth your weight in gold. And not just because those machines cost twenty thousand dollars."

She snorted. "I think your gratitude has more to do with Marisol and it being two days before Easter."

"How right you are." Grant ducked his head as Gabriel ran a chubby hand through his dad's hair. It stood up straight on one side and Kassey giggled at the sight.

"Your baby is fixing your hair," she told Grant.

"He likes to do that. He's trying to make me into a rock star." Grant pretended to devour Gabriel's hand and the little boy giggled.

"My aunt says mohawks are weird," Kassey went on.

"No way," Jack said, pretending to be astonished.

Gabby giggled and nudged her sister.

Jack raised an eyebrow at them. "You think I should try one?"

"No," she said, her voice soft. "Not that. What you said, my aunt doesn't let us say that. She says we use too much slang, like her friend Maya."

"No way!" He opened his eyes wide. The girls responded with muffled laughter and delighted grins.

Sabrina's face was pinker than before, if possible. "They're making me sound like a tyrant."

"Not at all. My grandmother hates slang, so I can understand those rules."

"Gabriel, there you are." Marisol came toward the group, arms outstretched. The little boy held out his hands in response and Grant passed him over to be covered in kisses. "There's my boy. So big, so tall!"

Grant tilted his head at them and whispered loudly, "I never get any attention anymore. It's Gabriel this and Gabriel that. Like I don't even exist."

"*Mentiroso,* I give you lots of attention. And you ignore me. I tell you to cut your hair last week and you don't listen." She turned a critical gaze on him and clucked her tongue. Gabriel giggled at the sound and held a small hand to her mouth.

"Calista likes it a bit long in the back," Grant said, shrugging.

"And that's what happens when you get married." Jack ran a hand through his own dark hair, cut short on the side and just a bit longer in the front. As active as he was, he didn't want to have to fuss with his hair all the time. "You don't even get to choose your own haircut."

"Is that why you date every girl in town?" Marisol's tone was light but her eyes missed nothing. "Always dating, never married. One date and then the girl is just a friend. Why? You like your hair so much? When you are old and it all falls out, then you will have no wife and no hair, either."

Surprised laughter burst from Sabrina and she tried to cover it with a cough.

"I just haven't found the right one, Mari. I admit, I'm picky." That, and he was never sure if they liked him for who he was, or the fact he was the vice president of Colorado Supplements. "But I can never have too many friends, right?"

"Friends, friends." Marisol's dark eyes rolled heavenward. "There are better things than friends. Look at this baby. I'm sure your parents are waiting for grandchildren."

"Well, Evie and Gavin can help them out there." He tried not to look concerned. And he wasn't, really. His parents had never really seemed excited about grandchildren. He glanced at Sabrina and saw her smile had slipped a bit. Marisol was making him out to be some sort of playboy who was determined never to have a family of his own.

Grant lifted a finger as if to halt the back-and-forth. "Marisol, is Easter brunch on schedule? Or should we put it back a week? We can still have the Easter egg hunt after the service, of course."

"No, everything is going to be fine. I am so happy all the kids will have Easter. Sweet little ones. Such joy." Her tanned face creased with a peaceful smile.

"Watching Sabrina work was absolutely impressive," Jack said. "We should get rid of that old statue out front and put up a monument to Sabrina the mechanic. It would be much more inspiring."

He felt his grin falter as he caught sight of Sabrina's face. The look she was giving him was a few levels short of overwhelming gratitude. Did she think he was being sarcastic? He was teasing about the statue, but he'd meant his original compliment to be taken seriously. She locked eyes with him and one slim eyebrow arched.

Not knowing what else to say, Jack tried to look as innocent as possible. Those beautiful brown eyes narrowed. He wasn't making it better. He didn't quite understand the emotions that crossed her face, but he wanted to, more than he had wanted anything in a long time. Something about this dark-eyed woman with the soft accent tugged at him. The noise in the gym seemed to fade away as their gazes held.

He cleared his throat and looked away. No matter how intriguing she was, he didn't have the freedom to do anything about it. His life was a complicated mess. With his dad recovering from his heart attack, Jack needed to focus on the family company. Plus, he was having a little professional crisis of his own. A woman like Sabrina wouldn't give a minute of her time to a man who didn't even know whether he wanted to quit his own job or not. Maybe after he was sure the company was on track, his dad was back at the helm and he'd solved his own personal problems, he could ask her to dinner. But not now, not yet.

She couldn't figure this guy out. On the outside he was just like all the rich, privileged kids she'd known in high school. He had the confidence that came with knowing whatever he tried would be a success. Guys like Jack were born halfway to the finish line and no one questioned that they would do well in life. Girls like Sabrina were born already late for the race.

But what she saw in Jack's eyes was something totally different. When he'd said she was impressive, she was sure he'd been making fun of her. Not that she cared. She was used to the snide comments and wisecracks over being a woman mechanic. She'd started to give him the death stare…and realized he'd been paying her a compliment. All her anger slid into a mass of confusion. This guy, who looked like so many guys she'd known and avoided like the plague, might just be different. In the space of one hour, he had found out more about her than anyone else she'd met in the past few years. She spent her time trying to keep her private life out of the way, out of sight. He certainly cared enough to talk to her like a human being. Was she becoming one of those people who made snap judgments, just on appearance? Sabrina hated being pigeonholed just because she was Hispanic and a woman, but maybe she was just as guilty as everyone else.

"I'm glad Easter brunch will happen." It wasn't quite a thank-you for the compliment, but it would have to do. As she spoke, her heart felt as though it was lifting, expanding.

"You saved Easter, *mija*," Marisol said.

"I'm telling you, the girl needs her own mural. At the very least, a plaque," Jack said. That teasing grin appeared again and suddenly Sabrina couldn't help wishing, just for a moment, that she was the kind of girl he might be interested in asking out on a date. In the next moment, she forced herself back to reality. It was ridiculous to spend a second dreaming about Jack. Even if they weren't from the opposite ends of the cultural spectrum, she couldn't be anybody's girlfriend right now. Kassey and Gabby came first. Full stop.

Grabbing her toolbox, she brushed back her hair with a free hand. "It's late and the girls need to get to bed. We'll get these forms back to you. See you next Thursday." She turned on her heel.

"Wait!" Jack's voice made her pause midstep. "Aren't you coming to Easter brunch? You fixed the Hobart. You should be here to enjoy the feast."

Sabrina frowned. They must look like all the other mission residents, sort of scraggly and poor. She self-consciously touched her ponytail. It had been years since she'd had her hair professionally cut. She scoured the secondhand shops, trying to keep the girls looking tidy even if they didn't have new clothes. Or maybe he thought they didn't have anywhere else to go because they were a broken family. Sabrina glanced down into the hopeful eyes of her nieces and let out a breath. As much as she wanted to deny it, he was right. They *didn't* have anywhere to go. Mrs. Guzman from upstairs was going to her daughter's house for Easter and this little family would be all alone.

"Sure, we'll be here," she said. The girls gripped her arms and squealed with excitement. Sabrina rolled her eyes at their response but couldn't help smiling a little. It was a homeless mission, but it was the friendliest place she'd been in a long time. It wouldn't hurt to spend Easter here if it made them happy.

"Wonderful," Grant said. "There's always room for more at the table."

Marisol beamed at Jack. "I forgive you for wanting to be everyone's friend. You help bring us all together for Easter."

"Glad to help." Jack was speaking to Marisol, but his gaze was on Sabrina. He rocked back on his heels for a second, looking pleased with himself. It made him look about five years old and it was absolutely adorable.

Sabrina forced herself to turn away, calling a farewell over her shoulder. It was nice to think of spending Easter somewhere other than their apartment and even nicer not to have to worry about finding something special to cook on their nonexistent budget. They would go to the early service, have a great meal at the mission, say hi to Marisol and the girls could feel as if it had been a real Easter.

She wouldn't have to worry about navigating around Jack and his heart-stopping smile because people like him didn't celebrate Easter in a shelter. He would be surrounded by family—parents and siblings and grandparents. If only it could be that way for the two little girls who trailed behind her on the way out of the gym. Sabrina's stomach twisted a little at the thought and she brushed off the jealousy.

But she'd had her fill of *if-only* moments and she was determined that Kassey and Gabby would be able to depend on her, not someone with her head in the clouds. She would show the judge that she was stable and loving enough to be their legal guardian, and they would be a permanent family. It wasn't perfect—these sweet girls should have a mom and a dad—but Sabrina would have to do. She was all they had. She would do everything in her power to keep them all together, to raise them in faith and shower them with love.

Any gaps left over, God would have to step in. There wasn't anybody else.

Chapter Three

"Hold on. I thought you were quitting as soon as Dad was well enough to come back full-time." Evie sat up ramrod straight in the chair across from her twin and arched a brow. Jack knew that look and pretended he didn't see it.

The morning sun was blazing through the window and the office seemed about ten degrees too warm. Jack pulled at his tie, wishing he was on Wolf Mountain at that very minute. It had snowed four inches that morning, and the boarding on Horseshoe Bowl would be phenomenal. But he was being good and was at work, like a responsible man.

"I am. Just not quite yet. I'm playing it by ear." His mahogany desk was polished so brightly he could see his reflection. He shuffled a few papers.

"Not yet? You've been unhappily employed for five long years, planned the big exit, plotted out a new business venture and now it's *not yet*?" She leaned forward. "Getting cold feet? I'll be there. Gavin will be there. You won't have to do this alone."

"Thank you." He meant it. Evie was closer to him

than any other person, and he couldn't think of making such a huge change without her input. "But I had a sort of revelation and think I should give it another try."

There was a small pause. She looked as if she was choosing her words. "May I ask how this revelation came about?"

Jack snorted. Leave it to her to cut to the chase. Not the why, but the how. "Just talking to a friend yesterday and I realized that I had always treated this job like it was an option, not a necessity."

She shook her head, dark hair the color of his own brushing her shoulders, blue eyes the same shade as his narrowed in thought. "We'll get back to that idea, but first, which friend?"

"A new friend."

"Girl?"

"Not a girlfriend." He waved a hand as if to say that was silly to even ask, even though he had to admit the thought had crossed his mind. More than crossed it. The thought had walked in and set up camp in a corner.

"Tell me about this not-a-girlfriend girl." She leaned back, arms over her chest. She managed to look completely uninterested, but he knew her better than that. She was going to get all the details, sooner or later. Probably sooner.

"The mission mechanic who was working on the chopper. Marisol asked me to help. We were just talking." He shrugged, hoping that would end the interrogation.

"And in five minutes you scrapped the plans you've made so carefully, for another, what, ten years of this?"

He winced. *Ten years.* The very thought made him

want to run from the office, out the door, down the stairs and into the sunshine. "It was more than five minutes."

"I want to meet this girl mechanic."

"It really doesn't have anything to do with her." Right? He stared at his hands, remembering the grease under her nails, the softness of her skin.

"Amazing. She must have really helped you understand this decision and be great at giving advice." Evie's voice was light, but she wasn't smiling.

He sighed. "I didn't tell her anything about my life. We talked about her job." Now that it came down to it, he didn't even know if he could explain. "It was more than that. She's taking care of her little nieces. I got the feeling there wasn't anybody else around to help. It made me realize that I don't carry a lot of responsibility, but I sure whine like I do."

Evie leaned across the desk and gripped his hand. "Just because someone else doesn't have the choices you do, that doesn't mean you have to suffer. I understand the guilt, I really do. But there are better ways to contribute to the world than by making yourself unhappy."

"I know that. But I wonder how hard I've been trying." He looked up, feeling the residual humility of seeing his choices in a new light. "Really trying, not just wasting time. I wanted to get some numbers on the production costs here locally and asked a few questions. Bob Barrows shot me down and I just…walked away, thinking of how soon I could get out of here."

"You don't have a lot of power, just a title. What else can you do?"

"I'm the vice president of the company. I can act like it for once." Resolve had been building ever since that conversation with Sabrina in the kitchen and it stiffened his back. "I emailed Bob this morning for the numbers. I want to make sure our local packagers are keeping costs as low as possible. The numbers have gone up for the sixth month in a row. Something's off and I want to know what."

Evie leaned back in her chair. "I don't understand how one conversation can make you rethink your plans. But whatever you decide, I'm behind you." She paused, biting her lip. "Just make sure you're not acting out of guilt. We can't help which family we're born into."

"But I've sure spent a lot of time complaining, rather than using it to my advantage."

Her eyes went a bit wider. "You've never wanted much to do with the family business. Now you're ready to take on responsibility? Maybe Dad shouldn't be trying to come back as president after all."

"Come on, Evie." He laughed but it sounded strained to his own ears. He wasn't interested in being the president of the company, he was sure of it. But he'd like to be a better vice president.

"Will this girl be at the mission on Sunday?"

He blinked, trying to follow her train of thought, then nodded. "I think so. But if you and Grandma Lili pounce on her, she won't have any idea why. What's going on with me and this job has nothing to do with her."

"I never pounce." Evie rolled her eyes. "I just want to meet her. Usually you shrug off criticism. It's odd to see you give so much weight to someone else's opinion."

"I'm telling you, we didn't talk about me at all."

"Then listening to her sad story gave you an early

midlife crisis?" His sister was a kind person, but she didn't have a lot of patience for whiners.

"I was already having a crisis. Maybe she just gave me some perspective." He rubbed his temples. "And sure, she's one of those people who has a sad story, but you have to pull it out of them. It wasn't volunteered."

Evie considered that for a moment. "Now I really want to meet her."

He blew out a sigh. "Fine. But let's keep our family business out of it."

She grabbed her purse and stood up. "No comments, I promise. I've got to get back to the paper and hear what the lawyers have to say about our slave-labor series."

"You've been chasing that story for years. I don't see why the lawyers won't let you run something already."

Her blue eyes turned somber. "It makes me angry every time they catch another group. It's always by accident, always just a few people kept against their will. And the workers say they were moved over and over, different buildings, lots of guards, rotating groups. We know it's big and it's here, right in our own city."

"Isn't there enough from the police reports to back up the series?"

She shook her head. "We can run a few small articles, and we have. But this series is different. It takes a lot of information from sources we can't identify, mostly for their own safety. The lawyers are there to make sure we don't get sued, but I sure hate having to take that advice."

"Do you think they'll give it the okay this time?"

"Not a chance." Her tone was nonchalant, but her

expression was dejected. "But I have to try. There are people in modern-day slavery, right here."

"I'm proud to be your brother, you know that?"

Her face flashed surprise, then pleasure. "Thank you, and ditto." She reached the door and turned. "Whatever you decide, I'm behind it. You know that."

Nodding, he didn't try to say anything. As the door closed, he swallowed hard. Theirs wasn't a perfect family, by any stretch of the imagination. Their father was distant and consumed by running the business. Their mother was sweet but distracted by anything that offered a spot on a committee. It had always been that way, as long as he could remember.

Evie had been his cheerleader, his confidante, his voice of reason when he got a crazy new idea. When Evie had fallen in love with his best friend, he hadn't been worried about losing either one. He'd been thrilled. Gavin was perfect for her.

He wanted what they had, someday. Sabrina's face flashed through his mind, startling him. Evie had asked a lot of questions, and not the ones he'd been expecting. Certainly not the ones he could answer right now. He pushed the unsettling feelings away.

He stretched his arms over his head, feeling the muscles burn, not used to sitting at a desk for hours at a time. Starting today, he was going to put everything he had into his job. No more soul-searching over finding his purpose. The fact that he was born into this family, and given this job, should be good enough. Of course, he had some serious catching up to do. Proving his value at the company would be an uphill battle after the years of doing the absolute minimum required.

And his first task was getting Bob Barrows to cough up those production numbers.

"But you said the rent change would go into effect on the first of *next* month." Sabrina struggled to keep her voice level, but her hands were shaking.

Mr. Snyder shook his head and spoke slowly, as if to a child. "You misunderstood me. I was very clear that the rent would be raised immediately. English can be a tough language to learn." He shifted his feet, shiny shoes squeaking on the polished tile of the apartment building foyer.

She was momentarily speechless. Sure, English was her second language, but she'd learned it almost twenty years ago when she entered kindergarten. The only thing she had misunderstood was Mr. Snyder's determination to evict her.

"So, if the rent hike went into effect right away, what do I owe?" Again, she kept her voice calm, as if she really had anything left to give him. Last month it had been a change in the electric bill that meant two hundred dollars for "upgrades." Then a few weeks later it was a maintenance fee for the small patch of scrub that passed for the lawn. Every resident was now paying fifty dollars a month for upkeep of the "courtyard."

"Two hundred and fifty dollars." He watched her face intently, his watery blue eyes barely visible behind the dirty lenses of his glasses.

"Okay." Sabrina felt despair rise in her throat. Their savings would take a real hit. "When do you need it?"

"Now." He paused, as if reconsidering. His long fingers fiddled with the zipper on his windbreaker. "But the biggest change is going to be next month. The build-ing is being signed over to a new company and they want a deposit."

"But I paid a deposit when I moved in! I have the receipt. Seven hundred dollars for a cleaning deposit and first and last month's rent. You can't charge me another deposit." She tried to breathe past the lump of pure panic in her throat.

"Don't yell at me. I can tell you to get out at any time." His expression was a combination of annoyance and triumph. "I'm trying to do the right thing and give you fair warning."

Fair warning…Sabrina put a hand to her eyes and fought to stay calm. All she wanted was to give her nieces a good home, somewhere safe and near a good school, but more than all of that was the need to appear stable. She couldn't be moving before the custody hear-ing. Tears burned at the back of her eyes and she gulped in a breath. But unless money fell from the sky, she was going to have to find another place. Maybe they could move quickly, so that they'd be settled by the time the court date came around.

She dropped her hand and met his gaze. "I don't think I can do that. So next month will be our last month." At least she wouldn't have to pay rent. But how she could ever come up with another deposit was a topic she couldn't even approach yet.

"You mean this month." His lips thinned out in a smile.

"I paid the rent a few weeks ago. I paid the last month's rent when I moved in." She ticked off the facts, knowing that Mr. Snyder wasn't being reasonable, but still hoping that this wasn't happening.

"Remember, the new owners want another deposit. Without it, you'll have to move at the end of this month."

Not even three weeks to find another apartment, to save up the money, to prepare the girls. Sabrina couldn't think past the gibbering fear in her head. She turned on her heel and made her way to the stairs. The blood pounding in her ears muffled Mr. Snyder's last words.

She trudged up the stairs, unseeing. Mrs. Guzman was watching Gabby and Kassey until she got home, probably letting them watch one of the telenovelas on the Spanish cable channel. A lot of shooting, crying, singing and kissing went on. Mrs. Guzman thought they were fun entertainment, nothing harmful. Sabrina thought they were tacky and sent a terrible message, especially to young girls, but nothing she said could convince Mrs. Guzman to turn it off when the girls were there. Just one more place in her life where she didn't have control.

She stopped on the landing and closed her eyes, leaning against the wall. Mr. Snyder was gouging the residents on the rent. He'd promised to give her a letter that showed the owner's change in the rental policy, but never had. What could she do to fight it? She didn't even know where to start.

"Are you okay?" A woman's voice cut into her thoughts and she stood up straight.

"Sure, just tired." She tried to smile a little, hoping the pretty blonde newlywed from downstairs wouldn't think she was crazy. Angie and her husband had moved in a few months ago and seemed to be wonderful tenants. Young professionals who had a dinner party or two, nothing too loud. They were friendly and polite, always saying hi.

Angie's husband followed her out their apartment, his brown hair smooth and tidy. "Hey, there. I saw your girls going upstairs today. They were giggling up a storm." He grinned, showing perfect teeth.

"Sounds like them." Those girls could wake the dead with their giggling fits. "What do you think of the rent changes?"

Angie looked at her husband. "Chad, did you hear anything about rent changes?"

"No. Nothing since we arrived." His brow was furrowed. "We signed a year lease, so I don't think they can change the terms."

"So did I. Mr. Snyder just said, on top of the electrical and the courtyard fee, there's a new deposit and a rent increase."

A long silence followed. Chad exchanged a look with Angie, then cleared his throat. "We don't have those fees. And I just saw him this morning and he never said anything about a new deposit."

Sabrina felt the blood rushing to her head. She swayed on her feet and put out a hand to steady herself against the wall. "Wait, the new fees, you don't..." She couldn't finish her sentence.

"I can ask him," Chad said, his expression serious. "There must be some explanation. You shouldn't be paying fees that we aren't."

Her shoulders slumped. No, she shouldn't, but it was very likely that she was. In Mr. Snyder's world, people like Sabrina didn't live in apartment buildings like his. People like Angie and Chad did, though.

"Sure, you're right." Her voice held no conviction. "I have to go pick up the girls. I'll see you two later."

She pulled her lips up in what she hoped passed for a smile and moved back toward the stairs.

She'd had a bad feeling when Mr. Snyder had made a new sign for the front of the apartment building. The old green sign reading Park Plaza had been reworked into something sleeker, more upscale. A bronze plaque attached to the building was understated and elegant, a visible marker of the changes the building was going to make, inside and out.

Mrs. Guzman had bemoaned the new fees but had already mentioned how she wanted to move in with her son and his family. Since Mr. Guzman passed away, she hadn't liked living alone. She wasn't the world's greatest babysitter, but she enjoyed the girls' company and appreciated their happy energy. Sabrina groaned. She hadn't thought of finding new child care, too. Moving would be hard enough, but who would watch the girls after school? Her working hours would be cut down even further. Sabrina had brought them to work a few times, to places like the mission, but it just wasn't appropriate to be taking them across the city on different jobs.

Oh, Lord, please help me take care of them. She fought back a wave of despair. How had everything gone so wrong, so quickly?

She tried to think logically. They had always made it through before. It would be tight for a few months. She'd have to pick up as many repair jobs as she could in the next few weeks. Her mind raced. Besides the amount of money she'd need and the few weeks she had to find a new apartment, it also had to be the sort of place the judge would think was good for the girls.

Pausing before she knocked on Mrs. Guzman's door, she inhaled deeply and tried to look as if everything was perfectly fine. Gabby and Kassey didn't need to carry this burden. She would have to find some way to prepare them for the move, but at the right time, when she was calm. There was a lot to do before then.

The first item on the list would be finding a place for them to live.

"Thank you for picking me up, Jack." Grandma Lili squeezed his hand.

"My pleasure." Jack smiled down at the older lady who seemed to adopt anyone within ten feet of her. He was thrilled that his sister, Evie, and Gavin had fallen in love and gotten married, but he hadn't realized that he'd get a grandmother out of the deal.

"Are you sure we shouldn't offer to serve?" Grandma Lili gazed around at the packed cafeteria. Tables were pulled into squares and covered with white tablecloths. The centerpiece on each one was a cheery bouquet of paper daffodils and tulips, obviously made by the mission kids. The place echoed with laughter and snatches of conversation. "There are so many people waiting."

"Grant said they had more than enough servers when I asked on Friday. As for the line, I think they're going to have us go one table at a time." Jack pointed at the corner, where a group had started lining up for the Easter brunch. The smell of mashed potatoes, biscuits, ham, green beans and pie was making his stomach growl. Breakfast had been hours before the church service and it was nearly noon already.

"Should we find a seat?" Grandma Lili started toward the far side of the gymnasium, but Jack put a hand on her arm.

"Evie said they had already staked out a place for

us. We just need to find them." How they were going to find anybody in this crowd was beyond him. And he had to admit that he wasn't focusing completely on looking for Gavin and Evie. He hoped to see another guest here, someone who had weighed on his mind for the past few days.

"Over here, you two!" Gavin waved an arm, catching their attention from across the room. He looked like his usual self, ready for a day at the office, except for a tie patterned with Easter eggs. Evie smiled at them from a table populated by a few older folks and a young couple. As the editor of a local paper, her work attire was often a black suit, but today she'd exchanged it for a light flowered wrap dress. Jack couldn't help but smile at the happiness that radiated from her face. His sister had carried a heavy burden for years, and Gavin's love had convinced her to lay it down. Jack would never get tired of seeing her like this, absolutely in love with life.

Grandma Lili and Jack made their way through the crowds to the table at the far wall. "You made me an Easter basket?" Jack leaned over Evie's shoulder and inspected one of the two white baskets. "I don't see a lot of chocolate in here. You know I love those little pastel eggs with the candy shell."

"Not for you, silly. These are for Sabrina's two girls. Didn't you say she had kids?"

"Nieces, but they live with her." He gave Evie an extra tight hug and kissed the top of her head. He hadn't even thought of bringing something for Kassey and Gabby. "And that's why you're my favorite sister."

"Better be for more than that, buddy." But Evie looked pleased that he approved of the baskets. "Gavin picked out the toys. He said we should only fill them with sugar if we want her to hate us."

"My grandson is right." Grandma Lili settled into the chair across from Gavin, adjusting the cuffs of her light pink silk shirt. "No mom likes what happens when the sugar high wears off."

"Speaking of Sabrina…" Jack said, letting the rest of his sentence go unfinished as he spotted her. He stood, unsure of whether to wave or walk on over. She had just come through the door, holding Gabby by one hand and Kassey by the other. The girls looked as if they were both talking at the same time, probably excited by the idea of the mission's Easter egg hunt after the brunch.

She caught his eye and frowned, brows drawing together. Jack froze, wondering if he had misunderstood their conversation. Hadn't she been expecting him?

"I'll be right back," he tossed over his shoulder as he started toward the door. Better to find out now if she was here with someone else. Evie could bring her Easter baskets over to their table.

Sabrina's gaze followed him across the cafeteria, dark eyes watchful. Her button-up blue shirt and jeans were clean, but worn. The girls were dressed in pretty dresses and sported matching daisies on their headbands. When he got closer, Gabby raised her hand and smiled shyly. "Hi, Coach."

"Hi, there, Gabby." He crouched down and held out his hand. "I'm just Jack today. Or Mr. Thorne, if your aunt insists."

"She doesn't," Sabrina said. Her lips twitched and she looked happy to see him, even though there were dark circles under her eyes. "I didn't know you'd be here."

He stood up, sticking his hands in his pockets. "Why wouldn't I be? I invited you, remember?"

"I thought that was sort of a general reminder, not an actual invitation." Pink bloomed on her cheeks, and she hurried on. "For people who didn't have anywhere else to go. I assumed you and your family would celebrate at home." She lifted one shoulder and let it drop.

Jack said nothing for a moment. She thought he'd invited them because they had no other family or friends…and she'd come anyway. That said more to him than a printout of her whole family history. He swallowed back the lump in his throat.

"My parents are in Florida on vacation and the mission is really special to us," he said. "We wanted to be here today." He leaned closer and dropped his voice. "I should warn you, my sister and Gavin's grandmother are the nosy type. Be ready to fend off a bunch of questions."

He expected her to laugh, but her eyes stayed somber. "I don't have anything to hide and no reason to lie if I did." The emotion in her face wasn't arrogance or boredom; it was something stronger. She seemed like a woman who was doing the best she could, with what she had, and she looked bone weary.

He moved before he thought it through, putting an arm around her shoulders and pulling her close. She didn't resist, but leaned into him. He could hear her shaky intake of breath and the slow exhale. She smelled like strawberry shampoo. When he spoke, his voice was rough. "Come and sit down with us. We've been waiting for you."

She nodded against his chest and leaned back. She glanced up once and he caught the glint of unshed tears.

He turned, wondering how a simple conversation had turned into something so much deeper. He wasn't a soft touch. He was as logical as they came, but something about her fragile smile spoke to a place inside, a place where you're at the end of your rope and only sheer determination is keeping you from slipping into the abyss.

Jack led the way, Kassey chattering about the Easter egg hunt and Gabby silently holding Sabrina's hand. *Please, God, Sabrina needs to catch a break. Let this be an Easter of peace for her.*

"Welcome, Sabrina." Gavin had stood up as they came to the table. He looked pleased to see her.

"Come sit over here with me," Grandma Lili said, patting the chair to the left. Her bright blue eyes were the same shade as Gavin's and her cheery welcome was the elderly, feminine version of his outgoing personality. Sabrina perched on the edge of the metal folding chair and waited for the interrogation. A single guy from a rich family probably had tons of girls chasing him, and his loved ones would be used to culling the candidates. But after several moments, Sabrina realized Grandma Lili was content to pat her hand and listen to the others talk. Relief flooded through her. Jack sat on her other side and she felt flanked by the two, as if they were protecting her.

She looked up to see Jack's sister watching her with a curious expression. Her gaze was assessing but not unfriendly. Maybe Evie and Gavin were the type to dig into her personal life. Sabrina stiffened her back and waited for the questions. She wouldn't lie, she had nothing to hide. But part of her wished that she was a professional who spent her days dressed in fancy suits rather than coveralls. She had trimmed her bangs that morning, hoping to look polished, but there was only so much you could do with a pair of scissors in the bathroom.

"These are for you two. Happy Easter!" Evie said as she handed the girls pretty white baskets.

"You didn't have to do that." Sabrina shifted uncomfortably. She'd made them cards and they'd baked special cookies last night, but there was no extra money for Easter baskets. Maybe it was obvious how very poor they were, especially since they weren't wearing anything fancy.

"It's my favorite holiday." Evie smiled in response, leaning against her husband. He pressed a kiss to the top of Evie's head and Sabrina dropped her gaze. Their happiness was so beautiful it made her throat ache a little.

"Oh, *Tía,* look!" Gabby was holding up a bright pink jump rope and a pack of crayons. Out of the basket next came sparkly pencils, a small coloring book, stickers and a special diary with its own key. A small bag of candy was the only sweet treat and Sabrina let out a breath of relief. They didn't need the sugar overload, especially since they still had cookies.

"Thank you so much!" Kassey threw her arms around Evie and hugged her tight. "I've never had my own crayons and pencils before."

Sabrina felt her face flush. "You have pencils, Kassey." They must think the girls didn't have school supplies at all.

"Not my very own, and they're not pink." She hugged them to her chest and grinned wide so Sabrina could see all her little teeth.

"Why don't you two color for a while until it's our

turn to get some lunch?" Grandma Lili took her paper place mat and folded it like a card.

"I hope they hurry. I didn't get anything to eat today." Gabby plopped into a chair and opened her coloring book.

Sabrina wanted to hang her head and groan. Gabby hadn't wanted to eat the toast she'd made because the crust had been darker than she liked. There hadn't been time to try again, just to catch the bread at that perfect moment of not too toasted. She wouldn't eat a banana and turned up her nose at the cereal. Sabrina had refused to let her have cookies, so off they'd gone to church and Gabby had skipped breakfast altogether. Now it sounded as if they had no food.

"Nothing at all?" Jack cocked an eyebrow at Gabby, daring her to insist.

"She's sort of a picky eater." Sabrina resisted the urge to list all the foods Gabby had refused.

"A supertaster, eh?" Gavin leaned forward. "Scientific studies have shown that picky eaters actually taste food more intensely."

Jack snorted. "In case you didn't notice, Gavin here is a scientist. Most of his sentences start with the words *there was a study on that.* He's like our own personal trivia search engine, but for science."

The conversation veered into medicine, diseases and which of them had the best memory for facts. The cheerful chatter was natural and affectionate. Sabrina felt herself relaxing for the first time in days. She glanced across the table as the men traded friendly barbs. She could have picked Jack's twin sister out of a crowd of hundreds: same jet-black hair, bright blue eyes, matching dimples. But within minutes Sabrina could see how different they were. Jack teased while Evie was serious. Jack chatted with everyone at the table while Evie was quiet. But something about the pretty woman struck a chord of familiarity. She had an aura of leftover childhood shyness, blushing easily when Jack teased her about marrying his best friend.

"I knew they would get married when Evie went up on Wolf Mountain with him. She hates the snow." Jack said this last bit as if he was sharing a secret with Sabrina.

"I don't hate the snow," Evie protested. "I just don't think it's really wise to propel yourself down a mountain on two small sticks. What if you break your neck? I can't watch you snowboard, either. All those flips and tricks. I don't care if you're the champion of the world, you're asking to break something."

"Champion of the world, that's a great title." Gavin grinned. Gabby dropped a crayon under the table and crawled off her chair to retrieve it.

"So, do you and Jack work together?" Sabrina asked Gavin.

Jack blinked at her. "Who, us?" He flapped a hand between himself and Gavin. "No way anyone would trust me around all those deadly viruses. I'm just a desk jockey in my dad's company."

Sabrina smiled at the term. Jack was the opposite of a desk jockey, as far as she could tell. He radiated energy. "It's wonderful you can carry on the family business. I'm sure that makes him proud."

There was a pause and the sound of silverware against ceramic plates echoed around them. The smell of baked ham and corn was coming from the next table.

"We should be next." Jack stood up, helping the girls

tuck the crayons back in the small cardboard boxes. His voice was light but there was a tightness around his mouth that made Sabrina wonder if there was more to the family business than pride. Whatever it was, it couldn't be anything close to her own family's sordid past. Undocumented immigrants, a father who drank too much and an unwed mother for a sister who'd eventually wandered away—it didn't get much uglier than that.

Jack helped Grandma Lili out of her chair and motioned for Sabrina to go ahead of him. Brushing by, she smelled fresh air and pine trees, and her heart contracted. When he'd hugged her at the door, she'd leaned into him like a woman who was desperate for affection. She hadn't meant to, hadn't planned on it, but as soon as he'd pulled her close, she'd sought refuge in his arms. As many times as she told herself she was strong enough to carry her burdens, a part of her knew she couldn't do it all. The fiasco with the apartment manager had haunted her sleep, stealing her peace of mind. She felt drained, beaten, weary.

Sabrina bit her lip as their little group made its way to the cafeteria line. Jack was a compassionate and tender man, but he was only being a good friend. She needed to keep her heart in check. Being supportive and welcoming was just part of who Jack was and it didn't mean anything more. If she was honest, she wanted it to be so much more than that. But men like Jack, from families like his, didn't go for girls like her. And the way Marisol talked about his dating life, whomever he did fall in love with would be the cream of the crop. He certainly wasn't hurting for romantic options.

She felt her lips tug up as Gabby and Kassey skipped

toward the line, pigtails bouncing. Those two were all she needed. She would stay in the moment, celebrate Easter and treasure every minute she had with them. They were a gift to her and she was thankful, so thankful to be entrusted with them. Everything else was peripheral.

As Sabrina took her place behind her nieces in the cafeteria line, she breathed a prayer of thanksgiving. For the next few hours she would try to forget about their dire situation and enjoy their new friends. It might be okay as long as she kept her thoughts on the road ahead and not on what she couldn't have. And one of those things was Jack Thorne.

Chapter Four

Jack bowed his head as Grant stood at the front of the cafeteria and led the group in a closing prayer. "Lord, we thank You for providing this meal from Your bounty. We ask Your blessing on this building, on all the residents, on our staff and most of all on our guests here today." Grant looked up as Gabriel escaped Calista's arms and toddled forward. The smile on Grant's face was mirrored by the people around him.

"That kid has Grant wrapped around his finger," Jack whispered as the mission's director lifted his son into his arms. He couldn't help laughing a bit as Gabriel reached out for the microphone and the last words of the prayer came in muffled bits.

"Amen," Sabrina answered and lifted her head. She had both of her girls by the hand and there was a look of peace on her face. As soon as she caught Jack's gaze, her lips tugged up.

It was the first time she had smiled at him that way, no shield, no worry. She looked so beautiful it made the breath stop in his lungs.

Gavin elbowed him. "Are you?"

"Am I what?" Jack hadn't heard a word Gavin was saying.

"Headed out for the Easter egg hunt." Gavin's voice held an undercurrent of laughter. "Hey, did I ever tell you my theory about this place? There's Jose. He'll explain it all." He waved an arm in the air and Jose changed direction from where he was headed toward the front of the cafeteria.

Evie was listening now, her gaze narrowing at her husband. "Oh, don't tease him. And it's not one hundred percent reliable."

"What's not reliable?" Jack asked. Grandma Lili was giggling and glancing at Sabrina. He felt as if everyone understood the joke except for him. And Sabrina, who looked from one to another with a puzzled expression.

"My theory isn't one hundred percent proven. We still haven't found anyone for Marisol." Gavin was laughing outright now.

Jose came up to their table and Gavin stood to give him a one-armed hug. "How's your wife and little boy?"

"Wonderful. And he's getting really big. Almost three and thinks he runs the world."

"We were just discussing the little problem at the mission," Gavin said.

"Problem?" Jose's face showed real concern and he glanced around the table. "Hi, Evie and Mrs. Sawyer. And a welcome to our guests. Nice to see you again, Sabrina." He smiled at her and the girls.

"Gavin is teasing Jack about his *theory*." She said the last words with extra emphasis.

Jack narrowed his eyes at the wide smile that crossed Jose's face. He thought he knew where this was going.

"Oh, right. The mission's little problem. Let's just

say it brings people together." Jose glanced once more between Jack and Sabrina. He seemed to think something was very funny. "Let me know how it all works out. But I think I already know." He waved as he headed back to the double doors.

"Can we go to the Easter egg hunt now?" Kassey tugged on Sabrina's sleeve and her dark eyes were bright with excitement.

"Sure, honey." Sabrina stood up, reaching for the dishes at their table.

"You go ahead. We'll bring the dishes up and meet you over there." Evie was already stacking plates.

"I'll go with you," Grandma Lili said. She slipped her arms into her sweater and leaned over to Kassey. "I helped pack those eggs. Go for the pink ones. I put quarters in them."

Kassey's eyes grew wide. "Really? We'll be rich!"

"Well, let's go, then." Grandma Lili took them both by the hand and they headed for the far doors, open to the grassy square between the buildings. It was chilly, but the sun was strong for April. Sabrina followed, a smile touching her lips.

As soon as they were out of earshot, Jack turned to Gavin. "Cut out the talk about the mission's *problem.* I know what you're doing."

Instead of looking chastened, Gavin gave him a punch to the shoulder. "I'm surprised you could concentrate enough to eat lunch. That girl has definitely caught your attention."

"Every girl gets my attention, remember? I'm the serial dater. I never take anyone seriously." Jack moved forks to a separate plate and reached for the knives.

"Right. Until now." Evie leaned across the table and

whispered, "It's okay. You can tell us. We're all friends." Her laughter was barely contained,

Jack rolled his eyes. "I don't understand why you've decided that she's the one when I hardly even know the girl."

"We didn't decide anything," Gavin said. "We only watched your face. It's like the rest of the table didn't exist."

He frowned, stacking the last plates together. Jack didn't want to be one of those guys who didn't hear or see the rest of the world when a pretty girl was around. He'd always hated the tunnel vision that happened to people in love. Sure, he liked to go out and have a good time, but it was never serious. And Jack suspected he had enough tunnel vision without involving a woman. He resented the fact he'd been forced into the family business, resented being given a top-notch education and resented being from a well-to-do family. Getting a good look at his own bad attitude had given him a shock. He was spoiled and now he knew it.

He followed Gavin and Evie to the dish area, thinking hard. He had a lot of work to do before he could think of bringing anyone else into his life. And one of the biggest tasks would be finally pulling his own weight at Colorado Supplements. No more half days or skipping work altogether if the snow was just right up on the mountain. As much as he wanted to get to know Sabrina better, for once he had bigger goals than fulfilling his own happiness.

"Did you hear, *Tía?* We're going to be rich!" Gabby bounced up and down, her seven-year-old body humming with excitement.

"Not really. I mean, you can find some quarters and maybe we can get a gum ball from the machine."

"Oh, let her dream." Grandma Lili giggled and leaned down. "Remember, go for the pink ones."

The two girls nodded, their gazes scanning the courtyard for telltale flashes of color. As Grant gave the signal, little kids rushed out to search through the bushes for plastic eggs.

Sabrina fought back a sigh. She remembered that excitement, thinking that life's problems could be solved by a nickel found on the sidewalk or a dollar received in a birthday card. "I just don't want them to have unrealistic expectations."

Grandma Lili glanced at her. "It's good to have hope."

"But it's not good to hope in something that can never come true." She hated the hard sound of her own words, but sometimes the truth wasn't pretty.

"Someone broke a lot of promises to you, I gather," Grandma Lili said. Her voice was soft.

Sabrina looked out at the courtyard full of excited kids and felt her heart sink as the memories, never very far away, rushed back. It was true. It was hard to see her nieces searching for plastic eggs that would make them rich, because she had felt the same way. Every time her father had come home announcing he had a new job and their lives would be better, she'd felt that joyous hope. And every time he'd been fired for coming in drunk or fighting or being late, she had known crushing disappointment. Her mother would cry softly as she cooked dinner, usually something cheap and simple, and nobody would say a word. Sabrina never wanted her nieces to believe in the impossible. It could only lead to heartbreak. Instead, she would make sure they understood she would always do the best she could for them, but life wasn't a fairy tale.

"I won't lie to them," Sabrina said.

Grandma Lili reached out and laid a hand on her shoulder. "You're a good mother."

"Thank you, but they're my nieces."

"I know." Tears sparkled at the corner of Grandma Lili's light blue eyes. "And you're a good mother."

Surrounded on all sides by happy laughter and the mission's guests, Sabrina felt her heart squeeze in her chest. It shouldn't matter what anybody else thought of her. In fact, it had been a long time since she'd made an effort to get to know another person. Her life didn't rotate around anybody else's opinion of her life. Unless it was the judge who could give her custody of the girls.

But she couldn't deny how good it felt to hear that compliment. She let out a breath. "I want to be a good mother, but I don't really know how. I don't have anyone to follow. I can only pray I'm not making the same mistakes my parents did."

"You have any questions, you come to me. I raised a few children myself. It's not an easy job and I don't have all the answers, but we can have a cup of coffee and a good chat."

Sabrina nodded, trying to speak past the lump in her throat. She'd always been the one trying to keep the family together. There had never been someone who would sit down with her and listen to her worries, her fears. For the first time since Rosa left, she felt as if she wasn't completely alone. Her sister hadn't been a good mom, but she had some good traits that Sabrina missed, such as always looking for the fun in every situation. "Thank you. Sometimes I miss talking to an adult."

"Just in time," a low voice said behind her. She knew who it was before she turned around. How much had he heard? The shame of admitting her insecurities and inadequacy made her face go hot.

"Didn't Evie want to watch the festivities?" Grandma Lili asked.

Sabrina glanced behind her and saw Jack, alone. His hands were stuffed in his pockets and he had a slight frown on his face. "They decided to help clean up the tables, but they sent me out to keep you company," he said.

Sabrina tried to focus on something other than his perfectly handsome face. He seemed to squeeze the air from the space around them, even though he wasn't standing very close. Maybe it was because he was so tall, or because of the somber expression in his eyes. She could tell he wasn't happy about something. She let out a quiet breath. It wasn't her problem if Jack wasn't happy. She didn't need to worry about making him feel comfortable. But a small part of her wished he would rather stand with her than be inside doing dishes.

"Oh, there's Lorna!" Grandma Lili waved across the courtyard to a woman in a bright red jacket. She squeezed Sabrina's shoulder and moved to let Jack in beside them. "Do you two mind…?"

"Of course not," he said.

Grandma Lili slipped away, zigzagging around laughing parents who cheered little children as they held up brightly colored eggs.

A silence fell between them. The kids were gathering at the far end of the courtyard, where Calista was handing out a few more treats for each basket. "I hope Grandma Lili didn't ask too many questions. She doesn't mean any harm." Jack stared out at the court- yard but his voice was quiet, just for her ears.

"No, she was fine." Sabrina shifted, hating the strange nervous tension she felt whenever Jack was near. "I like her." It sounded silly, but it was true. She liked her even though they had nothing in common.

"She always believes the best of people." The breeze ruffled his dark hair and he put up a hand to smooth it down. "Gavin works harder than a lot of people, and I used to worry that he was going to work himself to death. She made sure he didn't. She's got a way of see- ing a perspective we can't, especially if we're right in the middle of the situation."

She nodded. Her father had been someone who avoided work at all costs, but her mother had worked until the day she died. Right up to the hour she had col- lapsed on the kitchen floor. Sabrina should have told her to slow down. But she'd been busy with her own teenage problems.

Another long silence stretched between them and Sabrina wished she were the chatty type. It was hard to stand near him and wonder what he was thinking. Of course it didn't really matter.

"I'm glad you came today," he said. "I mean, you and the girls. They look like they had a good time."

"I'm glad we came, too." She watched her nieces compare baskets of eggs as they made their way back across the crowded courtyard. She couldn't help smil- ing at the glee on their faces.

"*Tía!* We've got two whole dollars! We can pay Mr.

Snyder all the rent money he needed," Kassey said, jumping up and down in her excitement.

"How did you—" Sabrina asked, her face flaming with sudden shame. It must sound as if they were behind on their rent.

"We heard you and Mrs. Guzman talking. We don't want to move, *Tía*." Gabby leaned her dark head against Sabrina's side and hugged her tight.

Jack stood silently next to her. Sabrina smoothed Gabby's long dark hair and didn't look up. She couldn't bear to see the expression on his face. She hated being pitied, hated how easy it was for rich people to be compassionate when it didn't cost them anything. Sabrina gritted her teeth. She wanted to deny it all and pretend everything was fine, but that would break the promise she had made to these girls. She would always be honest, even when it hurt.

"Everything is going to be fine," she said softly. It would be, one way or another. "Don't worry about anything."

"We won't, because now we have money!" the older girl said, her smile as wide as could be.

Sabrina didn't bother to correct them a second time. "We should be going." She turned to Jack. "Do they need any help inside?"

He looked exactly as she imagined he would. His blue eyes were shadowed with concern, his lips a grim line. "No, I think everything is taken care of with the volunteers." He paused, as if searching for the right words. "Sabrina, I don't want to offend you, but if there's anything I can do to help, please let me know. Times are hard for a lot of people and you're taking care of kids that aren't your own. I really admire you for taking them on. I'd be happy to—"

"No, really, we're fine." Her tone was ice-cold, but she couldn't find it within her to pretend he hadn't offended her. "For the record, you don't need to admire me. These girls are as much mine as they can be, in here." She tapped her chest, holding his gaze. "As soon as the judge signs the papers that give me permanent custody, they'll be mine in every other way, too."

He started to say something, a look of dismay crossing his face. She didn't give him a chance to go on. "Thank you again for the invitation."

As they walked around the building toward the bus stop, Sabrina saw Evie wave and smile, as if she wanted her to come over and say goodbye. Sabrina gave her a stiff smile and kept walking. It had been a mistake to come for Easter. Even though the girls had had a wonderful time, and the food was delicious, she didn't belong here. She had worked a few jobs at the mission, but she wasn't part of the staff or a volunteer. The longer she hung out with these people, the more it would be obvious that she was closer to being a resident than an employee.

Most of all, she wasn't anything like Jack. They were from such different worlds. His words rang in her head and she fought down another wave of anger. Part of her knew that she was reacting out of embarrassment. He thought they were a charity case, and it hurt more than if he hadn't cared to say anything at all. But another part, a deeper part, was furious at how he could have looked at her nieces as if they were a burden. Maybe he hadn't meant to, but that's what came out when he started speaking.

"*Tía,* it's so cold," Gabby complained, pulling her sweater tighter.

"I know. Let's get into the bus shelter and out of this wind." Sabrina hustled them down the block and into the glass enclosure. It wasn't much better, but the chill that came straight down from the mountains didn't reach into the very corners of the bus stop.

The girls perched on the bench and clutched their little white baskets to their chests. Sabrina let out a deep breath. She couldn't hold a grudge against Jack. He was their soccer coach and she would see him several times a week when they came to practice. It also wasn't Christian to hold on to a slight, especially if it hadn't been intentional. *Lord, bless Jack and all his family.* She would return blessings for injuries. It was the best thing for both of them.

The sound of the city bus echoed down the street and Sabrina gathered the girls at the sign, ready to board. She was determined to put it all out of her mind. Jack meant well. He'd realized they were having financial trouble and been on the verge of offering her money. The idea suddenly made her stomach twist. Her father would have welcomed it with open arms, because free money was the best kind. But Sabrina would never be like him. Being dependent on charity and leaving the care of her family to strangers was not something she would ever do. She would earn everything that she had and show her nieces that God blessed those who worked hard.

She filed up the dirty steps, ushering the girls past the driver and pausing to show him their bus passes. As they found a seat on the gray bench, she reached an arm around each girl and snuggled them close. They beamed up at her, still giddy with the morning fun. Their little family would never be wealthy, but they would have each other. Sabrina had faith that as long as she focused on the girls, everything else would fall into place. God wouldn't let them down.

Jack knocked lightly on the wooden door and waited for a response. There was complete silence from the office inside. He checked his watch. Bob Barrows had ignored his attempts to set up an appointment. The man never answered his phone. Here it was two in the afternoon on a Wednesday and he was nowhere to be found. The rest of the fifth floor of Colorado Supplements, however, buzzed with activity. Glancing behind him, Jack caught a young woman in a smart blue office suit watching him. She dropped her gaze and hurried away before he was able send her a friendly smile.

The whole floor of office workers seemed to be covertly watching him, as if he were a wild animal escaped from the zoo. He had asked every department for a two-month audit, hoping to be as prepared as possible for when his father came back. He was sure he hadn't made any friends with that request, but he'd been surprised at the lack of welcome. He didn't visit this floor very often, it was true. He didn't visit any floor much. But that was going to change.

Sighing, he turned back to the main area, hoping to catch a secretary who could deliver a message. His jaw felt tight and he tried to shrug off his irritation. Ever since he'd stuck his foot in his mouth at the mission, he'd been in a terrible mood. He couldn't forget the look on Sabrina's face when he'd tried to offer her financial help. Shame, hurt, surprise. The moment had played on a repeating loop in his head all night as he tossed and turned, unable to sleep.

He needed to focus on his job instead of obsessing over one stupid comment. All he wanted was the production numbers so he could cross-check them with last year's costs. It shouldn't be difficult at all to find that file and zip it through to Jack's computer. But Barrows was making Jack's job much harder than it had to be.

He strode toward the chest-high glossy black desk and waited for the secretary to finish her phone call. Her eyes went wide when she looked up and she nervously smoothed blond strands of hair back from her forehead. She was pretty, in a conventional sort of way, with sculpted eyebrows and a little too much makeup. As she ended the phone call, he leaned forward and smiled.

"Hi. I'm Jack Thorne. I was looking for Bob Barrows."

She giggled. Then she put a hand to her mouth, as if realizing the sound had come from her and not someone else. "I know who you are. You're the vice president. I've never met you, but I pass your picture in the lobby every day."

He wasn't sure how to respond to that, so he motioned toward Barrows's office. "Will he be back sometime today?"

"I'm not sure. I'm just a substitute. I usually work down in the basement." There was an awkward pause while she stared at him and he waited to see if she had any other information to offer.

Jack would have to admit defeat. No one had any idea where the man had gone, and the secretary was probably as clueless as he was. "Okay, can you leave him a message that I stopped by?"

She nodded, still smiling widely.

He wished her a good afternoon and walked back to the elevators. Heads bobbed up above cubicle walls and then disappeared, like human groundhogs. He forced a smile and hoped he appeared pleasant and calm instead of frustrated and furious. Life had been so much easier when he had only worried about himself and snowboarding up on Wolf Mountain. His father was coming back to work soon, after almost two months recovering from his heart attack. Jack had wanted to prove that he'd been a good steward, done more than sit at his desk and check the snow prediction for the weekend.

Punching the button, he waited for the metal doors to open. His employees didn't respect him, he had no real idea of where the company was headed and he was out of touch with everyone except his own small family.

The door slid smoothly open and he stepped inside, jabbing the button for the top floor. Volunteering at the mission had given him the idea he understood poverty, that he was connected to people who struggled just to survive. Frowning at his reflection in the polished metal door, he knew he'd been wrong. If he understood poverty, he never would have been so clumsy with Sabrina. He would have known how offended she'd feel. He rubbed a hand over his face. Of all the words he wished he could take back, the ones about her nieces were at the top. He hadn't meant it to sound as if he didn't consider them truly hers, or that she was only doing her duty. But it had come out sounding heartless and patronizing.

The ding of the elevator brought him back from the black cloud of regret that consumed his thoughts. The doors swished open and he stepped onto his floor, not sparing a single glance for the snowcapped mountains that shone through the large plate-glass windows. Striding into his office, he dropped into his leather desk chair and reached for the stack of production figures. He had made a lot of mistakes, but he was determined to start taking responsibility and applying his energy to what God had put before him.

He paused, a piece of paper in one hand and a pen in the other, as Sabrina's face flashed through his mind once again. Part of taking responsibility would have to include an apology. He hadn't meant to offend her and had only wanted to help. But there was no excuse for being callous. Sabrina was beautiful, smart and proud. Offering her money was the worst move he could have made, and when he saw her at soccer practice tomorrow, he would apologize. He had a lot of learning to do, and he prayed that God would teach him when to speak and when to keep his big mouth shut.

Chapter Five

The phone rang and Sabrina sat up in bed, eyes still closed. She groped for the receiver and mumbled into it. "Hello?"

A man's voice answered her in Spanish, "Are you the mechanic?"

She blinked, trying to push away the nightmare that still clung to the edges of her mind. Something about carrying all her belongings down the street, her two nieces crying behind her, knocking on doors that wouldn't open. "Yes, who is this?"

"Pancho said you were good with machines. We'll pay you five hundred dollars to come down here now and fix our equipment." There was a lot of noise in the background, metal clangs and loud voices.

Pancho Olmos? Sabrina knew better than to run off at the first promise of money, even if it was more than she made in a week. But Pancho was from her old neighborhood, a family friend. They had grown up together and gone to the same high school. She'd seen him a few weeks ago, out at the little grocery store that sold the chili-pepper candies that Gabby liked so much. He had looked just the same, maybe a little tired. They'd exchanged numbers and now she wondered if that had been wise.

"We need someone down here right away. We can't wait until morning."

"Where are you?" Even if she could get Mrs. Guzman from upstairs to watch the girls, it was still the middle of the night and there was no way she was taking the bus alone at this hour.

"Pancho can pick you up."

She noticed he didn't answer her question again. "He's there with you?"

In response, she heard the caller yell to someone. Seconds later, her friend's voice sounded into her ear. "Hey, Sabrina. I hate to even ask you to do this, but we're in big trouble here. I couldn't think of anyone else to call. We're on a really tight schedule and nobody else will come check out the machine." She could almost see him, dark hair sticking up in the front the way it had since he was a little kid, wiry frame hunched over in his big sweatshirt.

"But I don't even know what kind of machine it is," she started to protest, shaking the sleep from her brain.

"Label machine, nothing complicated, but we can't get the products boxed and ready for pickup at six if we do it by hand."

She took a breath and stared at the ceiling. High-volume label machines that were meant for round-the-clock usage usually had a lot of touch-sensitive equipment, computer panels and electronics that were outside her area of expertise. "I haven't worked with a lot of those, Pancho."

"Please, there's nobody else. Can you just come

look?" His voice was threaded with exhaustion. "We're going to lose this account if we aren't ready to ship at six." He paused. "For a friend? We were good friends once, right?"

Sabrina wanted to say no, wanted to say she had never really known Pancho that well, but it wouldn't be quite true. They might not have been friends, but Pancho's family had kept her and Rosa fed when there was no one else. She remembered how Mrs. Olmos had invited her in for dinner several times a week. She must have known how things were at Sabrina's house.

"Okay, let me call upstairs and see if I can get my neighbor to come down for a few hours."

She heard him release a breath of relief and warned him, "But she's old. She may not even hear the phone."

"Thank you, really, thanks so much."

"Better wait to thank me," she said and hung up. She sat staring at the phone for a moment, then slid off the bed with a groan. If she hadn't needed the money so much…no, she probably would still try and help Pancho even if he hadn't offered a lot of money. The Olmoses had been just a nice family across the street—they were good people, nothing special—but for Sabrina it had meant the world to have a hot meal and a safe place to be when her father was drunk.

Ten minutes later she was waving to a sleepy-eyed Mrs. Guzman as she settled onto Sabrina's couch. "Thank you, again. I'll pay you when I get back from—"

"No, *mija,* no." She waved a hand and tucked the blanket more securely around her chest. "It's good to help old friends. He was right to ask you and you were right to ask me. Now, go."

Sabrina nodded, realizing the wisdom of those

words, and slipped out the door. Pancho was already at the curb. His compact car made a rattling noise as the engine idled. She slid into the passenger seat and buckled her seat belt.

"It's not too far." He seemed nervous, jittery. His T-shirt was thin and the meager warmth from the afternoon sun was long gone, but his forehead shone with sweat.

"So, do you own this company?" Sabrina rested her toolbox at her feet and looked over at him.

"Me? No, I'm just one of the…" He paused and swallowed. "We do jobs for other people. This is a new account. Usually they're a lot smaller, with the crew just packing papers into folders or assembling products."

She nodded. It sounded as though they'd taken on more than they could handle.

A few minutes later, they pulled up outside an older warehouse. The four-story brick building was dark and the streetlights at the curb were out. Sabrina looked up the street and noted it was empty of parked cars. Probably the staff parked around back.

Pancho locked the car and walked quickly toward a side door. He knocked, glancing up and down the darkened street. Sabrina followed, unease rising in her chest.

A voice called through the door and Pancho answered into the crack, too softly for her to hear. Seconds later the door swung open and they trooped inside. A short, stocky man stood in front of her. He didn't introduce himself or greet her. She offered him a smile and without returning it he turned, jerking his head toward the main room.

Sabrina glanced at Pancho, but his head was down, his gaze fixed on the floor. She'd been in dozens of industrial work spaces, but this one felt all wrong. The fire doors were chained and the windows were covered. About twenty workers were seated in a row by the far wall. They were quiet—no chatter, no snacking or checking their phones. Most were men, but there were a few older women. None of them looked clean and they all seemed exhausted, with smudged faces and dark shadows under the eyes. It was the middle of the night and the night shift was tough, but their exhaustion looked to be the accumulation of days on the job with not enough rest.

The man pointed to the machine and said, "Fix it."

Any other place, at any other time, Sabrina would have at least rolled her eyes. Not now. She put down her tools and opened the lid. Her hands were trembling. His attitude, Pancho's fear, the darkened warehouse all said she was in a very bad situation. This business was obviously either packing something very illegal or these workers were not working voluntarily. She glanced at the labels as she started to examine the machine. It looked like some kind of diet powder. So the product itself wasn't the problem. A shudder went up her spine as she glanced over at the group against the wall. How long had they been here?

The stocky man stood near her, watching her every move. He was clearly the one running the entire operation. No one spoke in the room. Pancho stood next to the row of workers, not meeting her gaze. She wondered how he had gotten mixed up in this. He could leave, obviously, because he'd just driven out to pick her up. But there were all kinds of ways to keep someone enslaved. Sabrina thought of Mrs. Olmos and her kind smile, felt sweat slide down the back of her neck. *Please, Lord,*

*guide me. I want to help them, but I don't know if I can
even get out of here.*

The images of her nieces flashed through her mind.
What would happen to them if she never came home?
She had heard rumors, had known there were slave-
labor rings in the city, but she'd never thought she would
find herself in danger. She was a street-smart girl, had
grown up knowing what a lie sounded like even when
it came through smiling lips. Sabrina had always figured that if she worked hard and did the right thing, she
would be safe. But all it took was one phone call for help
from one old family friend, and she was teetering on
the edge of disappearing into the underworld of slave
labor. The image of Jack appeared in her mind and her
chest ached. She hadn't realized how much she felt for
him until she'd realized she might never see him again.

Sabrina sat back and wiped the cold sweat from her
forehead. The label machine was running smoothly
now, and she packed her tools away as quickly as possible. Her hands were trembling and she willed herself
to be calm. She'd kept herself from panicking during
the past hour by thinking of her nieces, their dark eyes
and trusting hearts. Her mind had come back to Jack
over and over. His smile, the tenor of his voice, the way
he made her feel safe and treasured.

The boss took a few steps toward her and leaned
in close. "Five hundred dollars, in cash, as soon as we
know we can trust you." His gaze never left her face.
"We'll be watching you. Pancho will take you home. If
we need you again, we'll call you."

Sabrina felt the blood drain from her face. She didn't
want the money. She only wanted to leave without ever

having to come back. "Thank you, but I don't do night calls. I just came because of—"

"You did and you will again. We know where you live, in that nice apartment with your little nieces." He leaned closer, giving off a whiff of stale cigarette smoke and sweat. "Sweet girls. Really pretty."

Her mouth went dry and she knew she should respond, but Sabrina's heart was pounding so hard that she couldn't speak.

Pancho took her elbow and tugged her toward the door. "Come on," he whispered. "Let me take you back."

She let herself be led outside. As the heavy metal door clanged shut behind them, she heard chains being drawn across the push bar. Her knees started to buckle and Pancho gripped her harder.

"Hurry," he said, forcing her toward the car. "Just get in."

She numbly put on her seat belt and folded her hands in her lap. The sweat on her face turned ice-cold in the night air and it revived her a little. As they drew away from the curb, she turned to him. "How can you stay there? You know what's going on."

His face was grim in the orange light from the street lamps. "I didn't know. Not at first. And by the time I did, it was too late. They knew where my family was." He glanced at her. "I've been trying to convince my parents to move, but they've been here thirty years. They don't want to leave, especially for no good reason. I can't tell them what's going on or they'd be in even worse danger. Even if they did find somewhere to go, I also have five sisters. What about them? What about their children and their husbands?"

Sabrina understood what he was saying but her heart

was still racing. There had to be some way to get out of that job. "Can't you go to the police? See if they can shut it down quickly enough to keep your family safe?"

Pancho laughed, a harsh and bitter sound. "They have me watched night and day. If I went anywhere near a police station or any kind of officer, they'd be on my family in minutes."

She swallowed hard. She'd struggled with her dad's drinking and her mom's health problems, with her wild sister who couldn't make a good decision and making ends meet. But she had never been in mortal fear for her family until now.

Minutes later they were at her apartment and Sabrina got out of the car. She leaned down to say goodbye, but the look on Pancho's face took the words out of her mouth.

"Sabrina, I'm so sorry. I didn't mean to get you mixed up in this. If we didn't get that machine fixed tonight, I was afraid someone was going to die." He looked at his hands, gripping the wheel so tight his knuckles were white. "I couldn't let him start killing people."

She nodded and slowly shut the door. Turning toward her apartment, she heard the car move away from the curb behind her, its engine rattling as it went down the street. Sabrina glanced up at the redbrick building, the shiny plaque at the front, the neatly tended evergreen bushes in pots by the main door. She felt as if she had seen another world tonight, a darker place than she could ever have imagined, and now she was part of that world whether she wanted to be or not. Along with the realization that she felt more for Jack than she should, there was a deeper pain. Tonight's activity was just one more reason why she and Jack didn't belong together, no matter how kind he was.

Sabrina bundled Gabby into her coat. "We only have a few minutes. We need to hurry." Her nieces were sleepy and slow moving this morning. Sabrina knew exactly how they felt. Her bones felt as though they were made of lead. Pancho's visit seemed like a nightmare in the cold light of the morning, and the only thing that kept her from crying was the thought of seeing Jack today. She had missed his teasing tone, and after the events of last night, her heart ached to see his smile.

"Okay, *Tía,*" Gabby said, yawning hugely. She let herself be zipped up and then trudged toward the door.

"Kassey, hurry!" Sabrina swept her long hair into a ponytail and forced herself not to get angry. They were just little girls. Catching the bus wasn't a big deal. It was one more school day to them.

Her oldest niece wandered into the living room. "I can't find my notebook. Teacher said we had to have our notebooks or we couldn't get a sticker." She shrugged on her coat and pouted. "I really wanted a sticker. I've done all the work."

Sabrina put a hand over her eyes for a second and tried to think. All she could see was the frightened faces of the workers from the job last night. She hadn't slept when she got home, but sat up between Gabby and Kassey's beds. Listening to their soft breathing and the gentle sounds of Mrs. Guzman snoring on the couch, Sabrina had fought back cold fear. Those men knew where she lived, and they knew her nieces lived here. She was just as trapped as Pancho was now. They might be moving, but there was no way to keep their new address quiet for long. People talked, especially in their little community.

Kassey sniffled and Sabrina's thoughts snapped back to the present. Notebook. It had to be here somewhere. "Get your book bags and I'll check the kitchen table." She ran toward the kitchen, hoping against hope. She could never figure out how the girls could lose so much stuff in such a small place. There on the far end of the counter was the bright pink notebook. Sabrina snagged it and hurried to the front door.

"Turn around and let me put this inside," she said, turning Kassey so she could reach the backpack. "And don't cry. Everything is okay."

Kassey turned and gave her a watery smile. "And we've got soccer practice tonight."

Sabrina couldn't help the spread of warmth through her chest. Seeing Jack was going to be the bright spot in a very stressful day.

Scooping up her toolbox, she hurried them out the door and turned the key in the lock. Outside on the sidewalk, she took Gabby's hand and made sure Kassey was on the other side. Her toolbox was heavy and she straightened her shoulders. So far, God had provided for them. She did the best she could and God had to do the rest.

The phone rang and Sabrina tucked it into her shoulder. "Hello?"

"Hi, sis!"

Sabrina froze midstep. She only had one sister. And that sister had run away years ago with some loser she'd met on the internet.

"Rosa?" She didn't know why she even asked, but she could hardly believe her ears.

"The one and only," she said, laughing. Her voice sounded high-pitched, nervous.

"Where are you?" Was she coming back to town? Did she want the girls?

"Oh, still in Vegas. Just wondering what you guys were up to."

Sabrina clamped her jaw shut. What was she up to? Only getting her sister's kids fed, dressed and off to school, which Rosa should be doing, except that she'd run away. Sabrina let out a breath. She needed to be calm and get as much information as possible. If Rosa was coming back, she might have a really tough fight on her hands when the custody hearing started.

"It's a school day. We're just getting ready to catch the bus."

"Oh. Right." Rosa had the good sense to sound a bit ashamed. She knew what she should be doing right then and it wasn't living the good life in Vegas while her kids were in Denver. "Well, I called because I needed to ask you for a favor."

Sabrina shifted her toolbox a bit in her gloved hand. "What is it?"

"Well, I can't pay my cell phone bill and they're going to shut it off if I don't pay it."

"Then let them." She didn't have the money to be paying Rosa's bills.

"But I need it!"

"You don't. You get a landline like a lot of people. It's a lot cheaper. Of course, you can't text on it or go on the internet, but you don't need to." Sabrina knew she sounded angry, but she couldn't help it. Her sister was calling to get her cell phone bill paid and it was the worst reason for calling she could have come up with.

She saw Gabby staring at her with a question on her face. Rosa hadn't even bothered to ask about her kids.

"I'm on my own now." Rosa paused and Sabrina could hear her gulping back a sob. "I want to be able to call the girls once in a while, if that's okay."

Sabrina could see the bus stop in the distance and for a moment, it seemed as if her whole life flashed in front of her eyes. She was always halfway to the destination. Struggling, fighting, never quite making it home. Tears clamped her throat closed but she fought them back. Rosa would think the tears were for her and she'd already cried enough for Rosa. The only people who mattered right now were the two little girls on either side of her, and the judge that would grant them the legal protection of being a family.

"That would be fine. I won't keep you apart, obviously. But did you get my letter? I only had the address that was on the birthday card," Sabrina said. At these words, Gabby's eyes widened. She knew who had sent a birthday card to Kassey six months ago. Rosa had forgotten her oldest girl's birthday, but Gabby had never mentioned it. That hurt Sabrina more than anything else—that Gabby had learned not to be surprised when her own mother forgot her birthday.

"I got it. I don't think the judge is going to let you be their legal guardian. You're not their mom." Rosa sounded bored, unconcerned. "But I'm not going to argue about it right now."

Sabrina let out a breath of relief. They were at the bus stop now and the shelter was filled with early morning commuters. She really didn't want to have that conversation in front of strangers. "Just so you understand—"

"I do. But…Sabrina, I really need this phone. It's all

I have left and I've applied for a bunch of jobs. If they cut off the phone, I won't know if anyone calls back. If I don't get a job, I'm going to end up tossed out of my place and then I don't know where I'll go." Her voice was rising in panic.

Sabrina thought of the people she'd seen last night. Maybe they had been like her sister once, just desperate enough to take a job without knowing all the details. She wanted to tell her that she knew just what it was like to be threatened with losing her apartment. She wanted to tell Rosa that she really didn't care what happened to her because the only people who deserved to have a perfect life were Kassey and Gabby. But she didn't. Somewhere, deep down, she still loved her younger sister. Under all her faults, or maybe because of them, was the little girl who'd cowered in the closet when their dad was on his drunken rampages. Sabrina could never just leave Rosa to fend for herself. She had always done everything humanly possible to protect her. Those habits died hard.

Sabrina looked into the eyes of her nieces. They looked so much like Rosa, with their long lashes and arching brows. The innocence that used to be Rosa's still lived on in them. Sabrina shut her eyes and inhaled deeply. "How much is it?"

Rosa mumbled a number and Sabrina's eyes popped open in shock. "How is that possible? Were you calling Liberia, or what?"

"It's a couple of months overdue. I've put them off as long as I can."

"How much is it just to keep it on for a little longer? Is there a minimum amount?"

"About a hundred." She sounded sulky, as if Sabrina was being stingy.

She clamped down the anger that threatened to give her sister a piece of her mind, whether Gabby and Kassey were listening or not. With the new fees from Mr. Snyder and Rosa's bill, there was just enough. She would have to take on some new jobs to make sure they had enough food, but there was always more work than Sabrina could handle. "Okay, but I can't give any information to you here. I'm at the bus stop."

"I need it right now. They said they'd shut it off today and I—"

Sabrina opened her eyes and watched the bus coming toward them, belching gray smoke into the bright blue sky. "I'll text it to you. Then delete it right away."

"Thank you so much. Really, thank you. If there's anything I can do for you, just tell me. I can send you the cutest pair of earrings they have at this shop here. They're gold hoops with—"

"Rosa, I don't want anything." Sabrina felt her chest tighten with anger. The bus pulled to the curb and they all got in line. She put the phone back to her shoulder, took their bus passes from her pocket and herded the girls in front of her. "If you really meant what you said, then you should make an effort to be in better contact with your kids."

There was a long pause on the other end. "Oh, right. I know I need to call the girls more. Sure, as soon as I get the bill straightened out, I'll call right back."

A teenager jostled Sabrina and she almost dropped the passes. She couldn't quite keep the anger from her voice. She was exhausted and the scenes from last night kept flashing through her mind. "We're headed to school and I have a job, but after five would be a good time." Did Rosa think they could stand around all day and wait for her call?

"After five. I'll remember. And thank you, sis." Without waiting for an answer, Rosa hung up.

As they shuffled down the aisle and settled onto the cold plastic seats, Sabrina avoided looking at her nieces. They were watching her silently. She tucked away the bus passes and got out her debit card. Quickly texting Rosa the numbers and the three digits on the back, she sent the message and sat back. Gabby tucked her hand into Sabrina's and leaned her head against her arm. She was the oldest, so brave and capable, but Sabrina knew Gabby carried a deep hurt from when Rosa left.

She looked at them, innocent and perfect, and wondered how Rosa could have thrown away such a gift. Sabrina could be just another single girl concerned with getting a date with a guy like Jack, but she had chosen her path a long time ago. No matter how much she found herself drawn to him, how much she replayed their conversation or the way his arms felt around her, her nieces came first.

They weren't a responsibility or a burden. They were pure joy to Sabrina. She would do anything to keep them safe. She was determined to have custody, but she knew it would be the best for everybody if Rosa could be part of their lives in a small way, because the girls would never stop loving their mom. If only Rosa could see that.

Chapter Six

Freshly showered and ready to coach a group of little kids in the fine art of soccer, Jack opened the supply closet and pulled the mesh bag of soccer balls into the gym. It had been a long day at the office. Phone calls, messages, meetings and other things he normally avoided at all costs were now part of his daily routine. And he still hadn't talked to Bob Barrows. Jack set out a stack of brightly colored cones and let out a long breath. He should be happy, relaxed, eager to start, but all he felt was nervous anxiety.

Sabrina would be here any minute with her nieces, and he needed to apologize. He'd been going over and over what he wanted to say, hoping to erase the hurt he'd caused. It was one thing to offer help when it wasn't wanted. It was a whole other situation to imply she deserved a medal for loving children like Gabby and Kassey. He hadn't meant it that way, but he knew it had hurt Sabrina.

He glanced over his shoulder as the gym doors opened. Gavin walked through, carrying a file folder.

"Hey, you're early," he called.

Jack waved. "Not by much."

Gavin jogged over, pulling off his sweatshirt and hanging it on a peg by the supply closet. "You're usually sliding in at the last minute after I've spent fifteen minutes setting up and corralling kids."

"Right, but that's when I've been rushing to get down from the mountain." Jack almost sighed. He'd heard there were perfect conditions today. With several inches of fine powder and bright sun, it would have been a great spring run. Gavin was his best friend and he'd know that's where Jack would have wanted to be.

"Evie said you decided to be a businessman, for real." Gavin shot him a glance. He was smiling, but Jack knew his words held a question. Everyone wanted to know why Jack was spending so much time at the job he'd always hated.

"Just thought I'd give it a little more time and effort, that's all." He shrugged. It was hard to explain. "I want my dad to come back to a smoothly running company. He's had enough stress to last him a lifetime."

The doors swung open again with a clang and they both looked up. Sabrina walked through, her toolbox in one hand. Her blue jacket looked too thin for the cold spring winds but her cheeks were pink and her dark eyes shone. He felt the breath stop in his lungs as she came nearer. There was such a confidence in her stride, such a brightness about her. The girls trotted alongside, their faces lit with excitement.

"Hi, Coach Jack and Coach Gavin!" Gabby fairly bounced with happiness, her long pigtails flying with every step. Kassey hung back a bit, but smiled widely.

"Hi, girls," he said. His voice sounded too hearty to his own ears. His gaze sought Sabrina's but she was focusing somewhere in the corner of the gym, her smile fixed.

Gavin held out a hand to Sabrina. "Great to see you. Can I put your box over here in the supply closet? I know those tools are worth a fortune."

"Thanks. I do keep a close eye on them. Either under lock and key or right next to me. It would be too easy for someone to steal and resell them."

Gavin took the box and tucked it in the supply closet. "I have a friend who works on medical equipment and he lost thousands of dollars in tools when someone broke into his car. Jack and I have the only key so they'll be safe here."

Jack straightened his shoulders. Before anything else, he needed to talk to Sabrina. Alone. "Gabby, Kassey, can you two put out these cones?"

They grabbed the colored cones and ran to set them along the lines around the gym. Jack turned to Sabrina. He saw the wariness in her gaze and hated it. It was his own fault. Gavin had done nothing but make her feel comfortable, but he only seemed to make her feel like an outsider. Easter day flashed through his mind. She'd been upset and overwhelmed. He had held out his arms and she had walked into them, as naturally as breathing. If he had had any hope of that happening twice, he would have tried it, but he saw the tenseness of her jaw and knew he needed to speak the words he'd been practicing for the past week.

"Sabrina, can I talk to you for a second?" He motioned a little farther away and Gavin took that cue to head to the opposite end of the gym.

Her gaze searched his face and she seemed unsure whether to agree, then shrugged. "Sure."

They walked a few feet away. She stuffed her hands into her jacket pockets and stared off at where Gabby and Kassey were setting up cones. She seemed to be bracing herself for another slight.

"Sabrina," he said. Then all his practiced words left him and he desperately wished to reach out and turn her chin so she would look at him. He kept his hands to himself and spoke from the heart. "I'm sorry."

She didn't seem to hear him for a moment, then she met his gaze. She didn't say anything, just waited for him to speak. Emotions passed over her face too quickly for him to track.

"I'm sorry for what I said to you on Easter." He sucked in a breath. "I was trying to give you a compliment and it didn't come out quite the way I intended." He watched one of her brows raise a fraction of an inch. "Okay, it came out all wrong."

Her lips moved up at the corners and it gave him courage. He went on. "As for offering you financial help, I hope you understand the way I meant it." The slight smile fell from her lips and he held up a hand, hoping to ward off another awkward moment.

She ignored his gesture and said, "Do you run around offering money to all the girls? Or just the poor Mexicans?"

He choked on the words he'd been trying to say. Then he saw her lips twitch and he realized she was teasing him. "Only the really pretty ones."

She laughed out loud and he reveled in the fact they were talking and not misunderstanding each other for once. "Fair enough." She cocked her head, her cheeks turning a light pink. "So, are we starting over?"

"Could we? Is that an option? I've never had to start

over before. I'm usually pretty good at this." He grinned down at her, wishing they could be like this all the time, finding the silliness in a simple misunderstanding.

"At what?"

He paused. At talking to pretty girls, of course. But that made him sound like a player. Maybe he did like to date around, in a very unserious way. Evie was always accusing him of being overly picky and never going past the first date. He wasn't shallow. He just didn't want the baggage of a relationship.

"At making friends," he said finally.

"Really? I have to start over quite a lot." She gave him a head-to-toe glance. "But I can see how you usually get it right on the first try."

She was flirting. He was pretty sure she was flirting. The realization made his blood pressure kick up a notch. In a good way. "Everyone has an off day now and then, I suppose. So…apology accepted?"

"Sure." She glanced over at her nieces. "I may have been a little too quick to take offense and I'm sorry about that. I just hear too many negative comments from people my age. I understand how it looks. I know it doesn't make much sense, taking on two little kids when I could be out having a social life."

He didn't say anything. He didn't know any girls who would choose being a single mom over living a life of dating and parties.

"But I've never been a really social person. It's not a sacrifice for me." She looked him in the eye, all teasing gone. "The fact that I love them and would do anything for them? It just makes it easier. If everything goes well, they'll be mine legally, but we've been a real family for years. We just need the paper to prove it."

"I can tell family is really important to you." It was a silly understatement, but she just nodded.

"It is. Maybe because I never really had the kind of parents that took care of me and my sister. We always had to fend for ourselves. Maybe that's the reason Rosa is the way she is. Maybe she just doesn't know how to be a mom."

Gabby ran for the far end of the gym with the last cone, its bright orange plastic shape gripped firmly in her hands.

"But then how do you know? It's odd that she doesn't get how to be a parent but you do." For a moment he thought he'd said too much, but she didn't look offended.

"By the grace of God." She glanced at him, her eyes misting with tears. "I wish Rosa would find her faith. I wish she knew how much God wants her to be safe and whole and happy, instead of running all over the country with different men."

She hauled in a breath. "When we sit in church and I look at the other families, I don't see anyone else like us. There are old people and young people and young parents with kids. But I'm not friends with any other single moms. I pray every night to be the mom they need and that God will give me a mother's heart for them."

Jack followed her gaze to where the girls stood listening to Gavin give them directions on where to drag the mesh bags of soccer balls. He'd been wrong. Sabrina wasn't just a beautiful, smart woman who fought for her family. She was a faithful woman who understood where true strength lay.

"If there's anything I can do…" His voice trailed off. He had said it once before and it had caused a rift in their budding friendship. He was afraid to say it now, but his heart wouldn't keep the words inside.

Her eyes softened and she nodded. "Thank you. I don't think there is, but thank you."

They stood looking at each other for several long beats until a voice called across the gym. "*Tía,* watch this."

She looked past him at her niece, valiantly trying to get the soccer ball near the goal. "Great job," she called back.

He wanted to reach out and brush back the strand of hair that lay against her cheek but instead he jerked his head to the stream of kids coming through the door. "Here they come. We should get back to work before Gavin gives us laps."

She smiled up at him and for a moment he felt as if everything was right with the world. He wanted to hold on to that feeling, never let it go. He'd spent so much time searching for something that made him feel happy. But life wasn't about being happy. It was about the people around him, and he'd never felt that more strongly than this moment, walking toward a group of shrieking kids excited to start soccer practice, this woman at his side.

Sabrina pulled the ponytail holder out of her hair and scooped her hair back from her face. She was sweating, tired and thirsty. And she hadn't had so much fun in a long time. Gavin was a master of organization, keeping the kids coordinated and on track. Jack was the team's heart, cheering the kids on, giving pointers and encouragement at every step. On a day when she felt the horrors and uncertainty of the world pressing all around her, this evening had reminded her that there were good people in the world. There was hope and light, and she wanted to be part of it.

Sabrina pulled her hair back into a ponytail and tightened it. Some people might say it was just a kids' soccer team, something to pass the time, but it had lifted her spirits more than anything in months. With what she'd seen last night, she'd been close to giving up. Life was too ugly, too hard, to keep on having faith that it would all work out okay.

And then she'd spent two hours cheering kids, showing them moves, running to retrieve balls and laughing. She had forgotten how good it felt to laugh. Her body was loose and relaxed. She worked hard every day, lifting equipment and yanking bolts from old machinery, so she was certainly moving around enough. She was no couch potato. But this sort of workout was different. It was about friendship and teaching and community. Sabrina couldn't wipe the smile from her face.

"Okay, everybody, we'll see you back here in two days," Gavin called out. "Leave your jerseys with Jack and don't forget to review your rule sheets. We need everybody to have the rules down before the first game."

Sabrina jogged over to one of the goals and started to corral the balls. Gabby was hugging goodbye to a little girl with a pageboy haircut and missing front teeth. Sabrina watched her for a moment. Gabby made friends so easily, but Kassey was shyer, more prone to wait for someone to reach out to her. Sabrina watched her younger niece from across the gym. She was helping Jack collect the jerseys and Sabrina was surprised to see Kassey smiling at each kid as he or she passed. Maybe this soccer team would be good in more ways than just getting some exercise.

"I hope we didn't scare you away and that you're going to come back," a voice said.

Sabrina turned, a smile spreading over her face before she even saw him.

Jack said, "Gavin can be such a taskmaster. He needs a whip."

"He wasn't scary at all. But I almost lost my head by flying soccer balls tonight. I may not be cut out for this." She had no intention of quitting, and the smile on her face broadcast that fact.

"Then I'll have to think of some way to convince you to stay," Jack said as he scooped up a ball and stuffed it into the bag. "I know running after a bunch of kids and getting sweaty isn't at the top of the list for most girls, but we really appreciate your help."

Tugging the string tight, she shrugged. "I'm not most girls." And he should know that. She spent most of her time covered in grease and wearing a hard hat.

"So I can cancel that shipment for specialty chocolate?" He grinned down at her and even though she knew he was only teasing, she felt her chest contract a bit. The man had good genes, no doubt about it. Those perfect dimples, bright blue eyes and dark hair combined with the easy athleticism made him almost hard to look at, but she couldn't help herself.

"Chocolate isn't my weak spot." She lifted the bag and started toward the supply closet. She felt him lift it from her hands and she let go. Normally she would shoot a dark look at the person who tried to take over something she was doing, but she didn't mind giving the bag to him. That set off a small warning bell somewhere. It was so easy to let him help her, even though she had never been very good at letting someone else be in charge. It was always better if she kept control.

"You're not going to tell me, are you?" He threw a grin over his shoulder.

"I could, but it wouldn't help you any. It's not something you can walk down the block and find in any store."

They stopped in front of the supply closet and he took a set of keys from his pocket. "Now I'm really curious."

Sabrina couldn't help laughing. He made it seem as if he really needed to know her deepest desires. "It's not that interesting."

"Then tell me. Cupcakes? Shoes? Sparkly pink stickers to put on your hard hat?"

From anyone else, she would have just rolled her eyes and walked away, but he knew it was none of those things.

He cocked his head. "Oh, maybe a special tool? Something no one else has?"

"We all use pretty much the same stuff." She glanced back at the gym. Most of the kids were gone and Gavin was pointing out the row of chairs pushed to the side. The girls were busy sliding them into place, Gabby working as quickly as possible and Kassey taking her sweet time to place each chair in a perfect line. They would need to bring back the tables so Marisol and the kitchen crew could be ready for breakfast.

She looked up at him and blinked. He was waiting patiently. He wasn't going to let her walk away without spilling her secret. "You'll think it's really weird," she said.

"Even better."

She chewed her lip for a moment, trying not to laugh. It was silly to make such a big deal out of telling him her little hobby, but it was personal, and it had been a long time since anyone had cared about her enough to ask what she did when she wasn't working or taking care of the kids.

"I have this thing about maps," she started to say. She watched his eyes widen a bit and rushed on. "Especially old maps. I mean, I like them all, even the new city maps. But I love looking at a place from a hundred years ago and wondering about the people who lived here."

"Maps of Denver?"

"Anywhere. I like them all." She wrapped her arms around her middle. She could almost smell the dust and feel the parchment under her fingers. "From other countries, the other side of the world, anywhere. I like how the cities in Europe are built around the square, so they circle outward like ripples in a pond. I like how the American cities are so organized in little grids, with streets named after presidents and trees."

"So you collect and frame them?" He looked confused.

"No, I don't frame them. I look at them." She swept her hands out in front of her. "Late at night, I get them out and lay heavy books on the corners and just…"

"Look at them," he finished for her. The edges of his lips were twitching.

"You think that's silly," she said, brushing past him to the supply closet door. He hadn't opened it yet, but she couldn't look up and see him laughing at her. She should never have told him. It was a stupid little hobby she'd started as a kid when her dad brought home a torn-up map he'd found in a Dumpster.

"I think it's great." He reached past her and unlocked the door.

She didn't answer, keeping her face turned away. Maybe he was serious. Maybe he wasn't. She didn't have the courage to look up and see which it was.

He touched her elbow, turning her to him. "Really, I do."

Looking into his eyes, Sabrina knew he was telling the truth. "Okay, but now that I've told you my weird pastime, you have to tell me something about you. It's only fair."

He grinned and tossed the mesh bag into the supply closet. "What you see is what you get. I'm completely uninteresting."

"Hmm. Not buying that. You're the vice president of a business, but you work on the financial board at a homeless mission. You're not married and don't have children of your own, but you like coaching a kids' soccer team. You have a desk job but would rather be up on the mountain. None of those things really go together."

"Well, when you say it like that…" He laughed, but there was a note of surprise in his tone.

"So, what is it?"

"What's what?"

"Your weird little hobby. I told you mine." She fixed him with a look. She wasn't going to let him shrug off her question. Maybe she was getting even, but deep down, she knew she was mostly curious. Curious about this man who could get her to open up when she really should have been locking herself up tight, far away from any man who would complicate her life more than it already was.

He watched Gavin pulling tables from the wall and

seemed undecided whether to answer or go help. "You'll laugh."

"Is it weirder than studying old maps?" She pretended to reconsider. "Maybe I don't want to know. Right now I sort of like you. If you tell me your big secret, I may change my mind."

He met her eyes and one eyebrow went up a fraction. "Do you, now?" His voice was a lazy drawl.

Sabrina's cheeks went hot. They stood, gazes locked. She could feel a buffer of warmth between them and the sound of the chairs being pushed across the gym faded away.

He leaned closer. "I like to cook," he said.

"That's it?" She couldn't believe he'd made such a big deal out of a little bit of cooking. "I know guys who like to cook. It's not unheard of in the modern world, Mr. Thorne."

"I really, really like to cook. I watch the cooking shows. I collect cookbooks. I probably have a hundred, at least. I take cooking classes every fall. I have a selection of cooking gadgets that would put a French chef to shame."

"So…not just a little hobby." She was trying to reconcile this revelation with the tall, athletic man in front of her. A vision of him in a chef's hat and apron flashed before her, but she couldn't make it stick.

"No. Do you want to know my area of expertise?"

"I'm sort of afraid to ask," she said, laughing.

He dropped his voice. "I make the best cupcakes you'll ever eat. I have mastered the art of the chocolate-fudge-with-raspberry-filling cupcake. I have won over enemies with my French-vanilla-orange-zest-buttercream cupcakes."

Sabrina snorted, less at the idea of Jack wielding an oven mitt than the theatrical way he was listing his cupcake prowess. He was poking fun at himself and bragging at the same time, and she couldn't keep from giggling.

He went on. "I have eased awkward business meetings with my dark-chocolate-espresso frosting and wooed women with my salted-caramel-topped mocha cupcakes."

A vision flitted before her eyes of Jack offering a perfect little confection to a girl she imagined was tall and blonde. Her stomach twisted at the thought. "Well, that's a handy talent. Too bad it doesn't work on everybody." She shrugged and reached inside the supply closet for her toolbox. It was time to be getting on home. "Some of us are immune to cupcakes."

"And some of you have other weak spots. Like maps, for instance."

She fought back a laugh and shook her head instead. She wanted to get home to her apartment, where it was cozy and calm, where dark-haired men didn't tease out her secrets and then charm her with talk of cupcakes. The way he said "weak spots" made her heart beat double time, and not all of it was a good feeling. She didn't have time to flirt but somehow, with Jack, that's all she ended up doing.

Jack spotted Lana following a young woman coming through the cafeteria doors. A dark-skinned little boy detached from the group and sprinted toward his mom with a huge smile. He shouted, "Goodbye, Coach Gavin, goodbye, Coach Jack," as he went out the door.

"And Coach Sabrina," Gavin called back, laughing.

"Really?" Lana turned to ask Sabrina, just a few feet away. She was motioning to the girls, holding their coats in one hand and her toolbox on the other.

"I guess so," she answered. Her face looked tense, as if she knew they had been talking about her, but her chin was held high. She smiled. "It will be nice to do something other than work and dishes."

"Well, glad to have you on board," Lana said. "But Jack or Gavin should have told you that we can't have anyone working with the kids without being cleared. We'll have to get your papers signed right away and a background check done. I'm assuming you haven't had any brushes with the law or any illegal activity."

Her cheeks flushed and she shook her head.

"Oh, Lana, look at the woman. Does she look like a criminal to you?" Gavin said.

"Looks can be deceiving," Lana said, shrugging. "Let me go get those papers so you can fill them out at home." She turned her wheelchair around in one smooth motion and headed for the doors.

"I'll go lock up the supply closet," Gavin said and walked away.

Jack shook his head, chuckling at the idea of Sabrina being a wanted criminal. He opened his mouth to say something about the chances of such a thing, then caught sight of Sabrina's expression. His words died in his throat. Her jaw was tense and when she looked up, her eyes flashed with fear and anxiety.

Their gazes locked and he felt the weight of the moment press in on him. He had seen that look too many times. Gavin's sister had become a good friend of his, but Allison had a checkered past. She'd run away from home, made terrible choices, but then turned her life around. She'd also lived in fear of being exposed until a few years ago. Sabrina's expression was as familiar to him as the back of his hand. This was a woman who had a secret, and it wasn't anything small.

Gavin appeared, not seeming to notice the tenseness of the moment. "We're all set in here. We can meet Lana in the lobby to get those forms, if you want."

Her gaze flitted to the girls, and she nodded. Jack followed her glance and felt his stomach drop. Was the secret about the girls? Had the mother actually left them, or had Sabrina taken them without permission? The idea shook him to the core and he turned, striding toward the cafeteria door. Suspicion rose up in him faster than he could contain it. Perhaps Sabrina wasn't everything she pretended to be. Perhaps there was a darker reason for her to keep her distance.

He didn't know the answer, but he sure was going to do his very best to find out.

"Just sign here, and here," Lana said.

"Thanks," she mumbled. Snagging a pen from a stack on the desk, she bent over the first sheet. Quickly scratching out her signature, she handed the first one back to Lana. She caught Jack watching her intently, and her face went hot.

She'd never been good at keeping secrets. When she was little, her sister refused to share her secrets because Sabrina would blurt them out at the slightest provocation. And now all it took was the suggestion of illegal activity and last night's nightmare came back in full color. She hadn't asked to be there, had never wanted to become part of the dark underworld of slave labor, but Sabrina couldn't deny that she was linked to it now.

She couldn't risk her nieces' lives by going to the police since the bosses knew where she lived. Pancho had made it clear that the leaders were ruthless. Gabby and Kassey were everything to her, and she wouldn't put them in danger. Even though she was desperate, she didn't want the money, not from a job like that. There was nothing she could do, except pray the bosses didn't come calling for her again.

She met Jack's gaze and saw his eyes narrow. He couldn't suspect that she would be involved in anything illegal; that wasn't the type of girl she was. But the harder she tried to put it all out of her mind, the more ashamed she felt, until she dropped her gaze to the papers.

Gabby was busy chattering to Gavin about how many goals she could score in her first game. Sabrina had to smile, just a little. That girl had a lot of confidence, and for that she was thankful. But the rest of the evening had her reconsidering.

Maybe volunteering as a coach wasn't such a good idea after all. She didn't have any kind of future with someone like Jack, and she couldn't seem to stay away. Really, she couldn't see her future involving any men at all. At least for a while. She needed to figure out a better place to live, get custody of the girls, and then maybe she could think about her love life someday. Until then, she needed to keep the flirting in check.

Sabrina let the heavy door fall closed behind her as she stepped onto the busy sidewalk. She took a moment to inhale deeply, purposefully filling her lungs with fresh air. Her hands clenched the newspaper listing of apartments available, and she flexed her fingers, blowing out a sigh. She'd spent all day searching for a place for them, and there was nothing.

This had been the last apartment on the list that was within walking distance of the bus stop and close enough to the girls' school. The manager, an older woman with wiry gray hair and a ready smile, seemed kind. But the apartments they listed wouldn't be available for several weeks.

Sabrina had hated trying to explain why she needed one within the next few days. The eviction notice colored everything she said before and after. No manager wanted to rent to a family who was being evicted.

Sabrina felt hot tears fill her eyes and she angrily brushed them away with one hand. She had hoped it wouldn't come to this, but it seemed as if moving to the Mission was the only option left for her and the girls. She was a proud and private person, and the thought of everyone knowing how poor she had become was like swallowing something bitter. But knowing she had failed the girls was like a knife to her heart.

She started toward the bus stop, feeling sick with her decision. Tonight was soccer practice, and she would have to talk to Grant or Lana about moving in. Sabrina knew they would do everything they could to help, but she swallowed back a sob. This wasn't the way she'd ever thought her life would go.

Deep down, there was another reason this move caused her so much pain. Before today, a relationship with Jack was almost impossible. They were from two totally different worlds. But now, with the realization that she would be homeless, she knew any chance she'd had with him was truly gone. He would only see her as a charity case, someone who needed help or money, never as a woman who was fiercely independent. And that hurt more than anything else.

Chapter Seven

Jack strode down the sidewalk to the mission and inhaled the fresh air coming off the mountain. He loved spring. He loved the longer hours and the budding trees and the sight of green grass popping through the muddy soil. Add in some time with a beautiful girl and he was all set. If only that girl wasn't so wary of him.

He dodged a group of laughing teens. It had been two weeks since they invited Sabrina to coach the kids and she'd been wonderful. She was kind, enthusiastic and fair. The kids flocked to her even more than they did to Gavin. But when he talked to her, he still saw caution in her eyes. She had accepted his apology but seemed to avoid him. No more chatting about secret hobbies. No more blushing. No more flirting. He couldn't blame her. They both had too much going on in their lives for a serious relationship, but somehow he couldn't help wishing it was different.

Jack took a deep breath before he pulled open the mission door. The reflection in the glass showed that he was long overdue for a haircut. He tried to smooth his hair down, but the wind made it stand up again.

Jack crossed the lobby as quickly as he could without all-out running. The day had been taken up with meetings and phone calls. Bob Barrows had finally given him the figures he'd been after, but they made no sense whatsoever. He had been calling all over the city, trying to get it straightened out. The bills from the factories were missing, but the payments for packing the supplements were still going out. It was amazing that Barrows thought any of that information was going to be sufficient. Unless he hadn't actually believed that Jack was going to review the sheets, which was a real possibility. Jack hadn't been known for paying attention before.

"You're late," Lana called from behind the desk. She shook a finger at him but she was laughing.

"Shh, it's our secret," he called back. His dress shoes were slipping on the polished lobby floor and he slowed down before pulling the gym door open. The place was already filled with kids. Gavin was at the far end, directing pairs of kids as they kicked a ball to each other. Jack scanned the gym and found Sabrina near the wall, where she was tying a little boy's sneaker. Her dark hair was pulled back as usual, but she looked wan and tired. He watched her as he walked to the supply closet, feeling a warmth spread in his chest. It felt good just to see her.

She glanced up, as if she felt the weight of his gaze. He lifted a hand and waved. She stood still, her eyes going wide, then looked back to the little boy, who was talking earnestly to her. Jack tried not to feel disappointed that she didn't look very happy to see him. He smoothed his tie and hoped he didn't look like the desk jockey he'd become. It was hard to pull off the appearance of being a fun date in a corporate suit.

"Hey, you're so late I thought you'd decided to quit the team." Gavin walked over and gave him a playful punch on the arm.

"Never. Just got caught up in some office work."

"Uh-oh. Now I know the world is truly ending." He clutched at his chest and staggered.

Jack snorted. "Very funny." He pulled open the supply closet door and rooted around. "I left a bag in here… somewhere…oh, here it is."

"I hope it has extra clothes, because the suit isn't exactly standard-issue soccer gear."

He retreated from the closet and smoothed down his tie. "I'll run and change."

As he passed back through the cafeteria, Gabby ran up to him. "Coach Jack, where were you?"

"At work, kiddo." He squeezed her shoulder. "Be right back. I've got to get out of this suit." Over Gabby's head, he saw Sabrina watching him. He hoped she didn't think he was late because he knew she'd be here to pick up the slack. It wasn't that at all.

The practice flew by, kids shrieking with laughter and the coaches doing their best to stay out of the way of danger. Jack saw Sabrina speak to the girls, who nodded and ran to help Gavin clean up. Then she left the gym without a backward glance. Jack waited a few minutes, but when she didn't come back, he caught Gavin's attention and pointed toward the door.

"Be right back," he called.

"Not a problem," Gavin said, waving a hand.

Jack didn't have to look far. Sabrina stood to one side of the lobby desk, talking to Jose. His face was somber and he was leaning down, speaking softly to her. He had his arm around her shoulders and Sabrina was wiping away tears. Jack felt the blood drain from his face. This woman, who never backed down and never gave up, was weeping in public.

He changed course and headed straight toward them. She looked up and for a moment, he saw fear flash behind her eyes. Jack's concern twisted into dread.

"What's going on?" he asked.

Jose glanced at Lana, then looked to Sabrina for direction. "We're talking, getting things figured out."

Sabrina swallowed hard and looked up to meet his gaze. He had never seen her so weary, so full of despair. "The girls and I are moving in."

"Moving in?" Jack struggled to understand what Sabrina was saying. "Where?"

"Here," Jose said.

Jack stepped back in shock. His eyes went wide and it took several seconds to get his brain moving again. "But why?"

Sabrina shook her head, dark hair slipping loose from her ponytail. She glanced at the suit in his hand and for a moment, it seemed as if she couldn't find the words. "We just can't afford the rent and I can't find another place right away."

"Why not?" Jack looked from Jose to Lana. There must be something they could do. "We'll go out tomorrow and look around. There are tons of apartments open. I'm sure we can find something."

She was shaking her head again. "It's not that easy." She closed her eyes for a moment and Jack yearned to reach out and fold her in his arms. She was so sad, so weary. "The first and last month's rent plus deposit is more than I have right now."

"I can pay for that, it's no problem." He felt a rush of

relief. If money was the only issue, then they could be in an apartment tomorrow. He smiled at Lana, certain she would be nodding her head. She looked at him, the expression on her face difficult to define.

"No, I'll pay for my own place." Sabrina's voice was quiet, but the tone was so final that he felt the weight of her decision like a door slamming shut.

He ran a hand through his hair and tried to think. "You can't get an extension on the rent?"

Something in her expression tore at his heart. It was shame and anger. "No, it's not possible. I've done everything I can. I spent the whole day tracking down apartments, and everything that's open immediately is too far from the bus line. The girls would never get to school on time."

There was a pause in the conversation and the only sound was the echo of children cleaning up in the gym. Sabrina took a shaky breath. "I've thought it through and there's no other way to get caught up unless we move in here. Lana says they have a place for us in the family area."

Lana cleared her throat. "In the winter, everything would be filled up, but since it's warmer, we've got a place. It's small, just a single room for the three of you, but the meals are provided."

Jack swallowed hard. He shouldn't be surprised that something like this had happened. The working poor were everywhere, Evie said. They looked as though they were doing all right, but they were one disaster away from homelessness. And now Sabrina, Gabby and Kassey were part of that population.

"There aren't any friends you can stay with? Or family? Not a single person you could call?" As soon as he asked the questions, he wanted to take them back. She'd already said she didn't have many friends. And her parents were dead. The only person left would be her sister, who had run off somewhere. Anger swelled in his chest and he blew out a breath. It wasn't fair that someone who worked as hard as Sabrina could end up with nothing. Was there something else she was hiding?

"I wish there was," she said softly. She examined her hands, her face tight. "But it won't be so bad here. I know you all and Grant and some of the parents. It will be fine."

Jack glanced at Lana and blinked at her expression. She was glaring at him, as if he'd said something wrong. He backtracked over his words and realized how his comment sounded—as if he was blaming her for not having friends or a family to shelter her.

He reached out, without caring who saw, and gathered her to him. Jack held her tight, feeling the tenseness in her body, the rigidity of her spine. Within moments, she relaxed against him, burying her face in his chest. A soft sound escaped her and he knew she was crying.

"I didn't mean it that way," he whispered into her hair. "I'm sorry. It's not your fault." Even though she was taking full responsibility, everything about Sabrina said she was overly cautious and would never take risks. Something completely unexpected had happened.

She took a shuddering breath and pushed back from him. "I'm okay," she said, wiping her face with her hands. She didn't look at all okay, but he dropped his arms to his sides.

"I wish you would let me—"

"No, no, we'll be fine." She forced a small smile and turned to Lana and Jose. "Anyway, if I could fill out those papers at home and bring them tomorrow, that would be great. I'll have time to prepare the girls a little bit."

"Okay, so when do we start moving?" She wouldn't accept his money, but she might accept his help in other ways.

"We really don't have much. Lana says we can move in on Friday." Sabrina's chin was level, but her eyes glittered with unshed tears. He couldn't imagine how hard this was for her.

Jack blinked, realizing how stupid he sounded. You didn't move to a homeless mission with all your furniture. Something else occurred to him, but he was almost afraid to say it. "You said…you mentioned that you had a custody hearing coming up."

Her shoulders sagged. "Yes. Soon. We're waiting for the letter that will give us the exact day."

Jose said, "We've had residents go through custody hearings before. We can come with you to give character witness, if you'd like."

Sabrina nodded. "That would be nice." Her voice was flat and Jack knew why. It would be much better to show a judge how you lived in the same apartment for years than to bring a staff member from the homeless mission as a character witness.

The cafeteria door swung open and Gavin peered out. "I've lost all my helpers," he called toward the desk.

In the next moment, he saw Sabrina's tear-splotched face and shot a worried glance at Jack, then Lana and Jose. "No hurry," he said in a quieter tone and disappeared back into the gym.

"We should go in," she said. "Lana, I'll pick those up on the way out."

"I'll get everything ready. Jose will deliver the intake papers to Grant as soon as I get them printed up." The secretary wheeled around the desk and reached for Sabrina's hand. "It's going to be okay."

"I know," she said. But Jack saw the despair in her eyes. He knew that with the custody hearing coming up, things might actually turn out far from okay.

Sabrina stared up at her bedroom ceiling, her heart pounding. Something had woken her. The room was pitch-dark, the only light a sliver from the streetlamp outside, coming from the crack of the curtains. She waited, listening hard. Had one of the girls cried out in her sleep? That evening there had been a letter from the courts, giving their date with the judge. In three weeks she would finally know for sure whether she could get permanent custody of the girls. She had fallen asleep praying, as always.

A pounding at the door made her sit up in shock. She was out of the bed and throwing on her robe before she thought it through. At the door she peered into the peephole. Pancho stood outside, his face noticeably worried.

Sabrina stepped back. She didn't want to open the door. She never wanted to speak to Pancho again. He had brought a nightmare into her life and she wished she could pretend it had never happened.

"Sabrina," he called softly. "I know you're there. I heard you."

She put a hand to her mouth, unsure of what to do.

"Please, Sabrina. Please. They know where my mama lives." Pancho's voice cracked at the last word.

She leaned her head against the door. *Lord, what do*

I do? He's in trouble, but helping him puts me in danger. The girls need me.

"Please." It was just one more word, but the despair in his voice was too much. Sabrina threw the bolt and slid off the chain.

"Mrs. Guzman is gone. There's no one to watch the girls."

"You'll have to bring them." He was white and there were dark smudges on one cheek. She wasn't sure if it was grease or bruises and was afraid to look too closely.

"Pancho, are you serious?" She choked back her anger. "They can't go there."

He looked around, running a hand through his crew cut. The fingers of one hand were tattooed with numbers and Sabrina wondered what it meant. "They can stay in the car. I'll be outside with them."

"It's the middle of the night." She was shaking her head. "I can't wake them up."

He stepped closer, breathing heavily. "You opened the door. You knew what I needed. You can leave them here, sleeping, or bring them along. That's all I can offer you."

Her breath stopped in her lungs. Would he harm her? Was he that desperate? She swallowed hard. If she left them and something happened to her, they would be alone until someone came to check on them, or they left to go find her. If she brought them along, they could be hurt.

Sweat broke out on her forehead and her knees started to shake. She was going to have to leave them. And pray that she would be back before they woke. Her mind flashed to Jack and for just a moment, she thought about calling him. But how could she possibly explain? He would never understand how she could be part of this.

"Okay. Let me get my toolbox." Her heart was pounding so loudly her vision was blurring. Stuffing her feet into her shoes and stripping off her robe, she pulled on her coat.

"Thank you, thank you," Pancho breathed, relief making him sag against the doorjamb.

She grabbed her keys and walked through the door. Turning to lock up from the outside, she paused. Her hands were sweaty, her mouth was dry. She was doing what she'd promised she would never do: she was leaving her nieces. *Alone.*

Sabrina jumped from Pancho's car and raced for the apartment entrance. *Please, Lord, let them be okay.* It had only been a few hours and the sky was still dark.

She barely heard Pancho driving away from the curb. What she had seen tonight had been just as shocking, but no longer a surprise. The same group of people, the same arrogant boss with dead eyes, the same stench of fear. There was nothing she could do but work as quickly as she could to fix the machine. She was just as trapped as they were, and this time she had put her nieces in a terrible position.

Running up the flights of stairs, her toolbox banging against her leg, Sabrina felt her lungs searing with every breath. *Please, please, please.*

She was almost weeping with anxiety as she worked the locks on her front door and swung it inward. Everything was quiet. The living room was dark. She set the toolbox on the carpet and bolted the door, sliding the chain on for good measure. It wouldn't keep the nightmares away, but for now, it was all she had.

Creeping down the hallway, she peeked into the tiny room where Kassey and Gabby slept. The floor showed dark shapes where the girls had dropped toys and not picked them up. She navigated the room in darkness and leaned into the bottom bunk, reaching out a hand to smooth the hair from Gabby's forehead. Her covers were kicked to the end of the bed and Sabrina brought them back up, tucking them tightly around her shoulders.

The little girl sighed deeply in her sleep. Sabrina straightened up and peered into the top bunk. Kassey was there, hunched into her blankets. She laid a hand on Kassey's soft hair, whispering a prayer of thanks.

For now, they were safe. But something had to be done. She couldn't keep running to help the slave laborers, as if she was their personal mechanic. When they moved to the Mission, Pancho couldn't get to her in the middle of the night, but they still would have to leave for school and work. She and the girls couldn't hide in the Mission all day. She had become part of the business, another cog in the wheel of fear and silence, and that had to change.

Sabrina walked to the kitchen and sat at the table in the dark. She had to come up with some way to expose the group without putting the girls in any more danger than they already were. Otherwise, she might as well give up.

The sky was turning light at the edges before she finally rose from the table, her muscles protesting stiffly.

She had to find a way out of this nightmare before it consumed them the same way it had Pancho and all the people she had seen huddled in the warehouse tonight.

Chapter Eight

Lana waved from behind the desk. "Sabrina's already here. The girl is making you look bad."

Jack grinned. He was usually the one to help Gavin set up and now he was sliding in at the last minute. "That's nothing new, Lana. I'm getting used to it."

She raised her eyebrows at him and he kept on going. It was true—Sabrina made him look like a slacker, even though she didn't mean to. She made him want to be a better person and he couldn't fault her for that.

The gym was crowded with kids already. Gavin stood in the middle of the room, giving a talk to four little boys. Jack fought a smile. He recognized those kids. They had energy to burn and unfortunately that included never stopping to learn the rules.

Sabrina was helping a line of kids into colored mesh jerseys. She glanced up and froze, hands holding out a shirt for a blond-haired girl. Sabrina looked the same as always—ponytail, shorts, running shoes—but he couldn't tear his gaze away. She smiled and looked back to the little girl who stood patiently, arms up, waiting for Sabrina to put her jersey on. Jack was only feet away now and he saw the blush that crept into Sabrina's cheeks.

A flare of happiness went through him at the sight. A woman didn't blush for no reason.

"Glad you finally decided to join us," Gavin said as the boys scattered into the main area of the gym.

"Sorry. I had a meeting then had to run home to change. Plus, you have help now. I knew you wouldn't have to pull José in here to assist."

Gavin fell into step beside him as they headed for the end of the gym. "You're right, I do have help, and that's why I thought you'd be here early." He wiggled his eyebrows.

Jack shot him a look. "That's not happening." He didn't bother to say Gavin was absolutely correct in thinking Jack wanted to be here every moment that Sabrina was.

"Why not?" Gavin glanced back at Sabrina. "If Evie and I can make our way through our issues, then you guys should have no problem."

He nodded. Gavin and Evie had an incredibly complicated history, involving family secrets, newspapers, media and two people who had learned to forgive and forget. "Maybe it's easier to get around problems in the past than problems in the present."

"You mean because she's poor?" Gavin crossed his arms over his chest. The look on his face almost made Jack laugh. Almost. He didn't like what his best friend was implying.

"Let me say it this way…" He paused, thinking hard. "I have less of a problem with her being poor than she has with me being rich." At least he hoped that was the issue. Maybe she thought he was a lazy, spoiled guy who spent his days snowboarding instead of working.

To his surprise, Gavin nodded. "I can see that. She's proud. She won't take any help unless she's desperate. And I admire her for that."

"I do, too. But I also wish…" He shrugged. They knew there would always be people milking the system for all it was worth, but those people were rare, and the mission believed in focusing on the ones who really needed the help. Some of those people would only accept help at the very lowest point. He hoped that never happened to Sabrina, but he knew what a struggle it was to support the girls alone.

"We'd better get started," Gavin said. The next two hours were filled with shrieks, laughter and lots of flying soccer balls. Through it all Jack struggled to focus on the kids and not the beautiful young woman who brought such a light to the team.

"Thanks for helping again," Jack said.

Sabrina turned, fighting the impulse to give him a head-to-toe scan. She was a sweaty mess and he looked as though he was ready for a photo shoot. "It's a lot of fun. It gives me something to do other than sit around and worry."

"You do a lot of worrying?" His dark brows drew down. He couldn't imagine how she must feel, getting ready to move to the mission.

She mentally kicked herself. She must sound as if she was whining. "Yes, but it's my own fault. Everything can be going along perfectly and I can still find something to worry about."

He grinned and for a moment, her brain stopped

working. Those dimples must give him an unfair advantage in the world. No one could resist him when he smiled like that.

"We're opposite that way, I suppose," he said. "I always figure everything will work out. I don't waste energy on what can't be fixed right now."

She nodded and didn't say what she was thinking. Everything must work out eventually in Jack's life because his problems were probably whether there would be enough snow for the weekend's snowboarding. The next moment she regretted her uncharitable thoughts. She didn't know much about him, really. He could have much bigger problems than she knew.

"Hey, you two," Gavin called out to them, "can you go out to the courtyard and pick up a few folding chairs? Lana says the preschool teachers forgot them when they were directing some outdoor games this afternoon."

"No problem." Jack was already moving toward the door.

Sabrina glanced back at the girls, not wanting to leave them alone, even for a few minutes. The mission was full of good people, but there were also adults struggling with addictions and abuse. Sabrina knew enough about that sort of brokenness to never want to leave her girls alone. It was taking a risk that could turn out to be disastrous. She hesitated, watching them.

"Lana, can you watch the girls for a moment?" Jack called over. The secretary looked up and smiled, pointing to the girls and then to herself. Gavin walked to another row of chairs against the far wall and the kids ran to slide them back into position. He was busy and if he got distracted, Lana would be another layer of protection against the darker parts of mission life.

Sabrina felt a rush of emotion at Jack's foresight. It was the sort of thing a dad would do, if they had one. She felt her throat tighten at the thought. Her nieces deserved so much more than an aunt playing fill-in until their mom wandered back into town. To see a stranger take the time to make sure they were safe, even for a moment, left her fighting back the wave of gratitude. It didn't help to tell herself that he hadn't done that because he felt the girls were special, that he would have done it for any small child. In fact, it made her like him even more. Jack was just that type of man—caring, watchful, circumspect. The opposite of the sort of man she'd grown up with as a father and that the girls had never known as a parent.

She pushed away the emotional storm battering her heart. She hadn't slept a moment since Pancho had dropped her off last night and she'd spent every free moment packing their things. Sabrina gave herself a tiny pep talk and put the toolbox back in the supply closet.

He pushed open the far door and they exited into a small grassy area. Two buildings edged the courtyard on the far side. Sabrina inhaled the smell of new grass and looked around. A few folding chairs sat neglected on the cement walkway.

"I was teasing you, but I want you to know I really do appreciate you helping tonight. We both do. Gavin has poured his free time into this team and he believes that it will make a difference for the kids."

"I think he's right," she said. The sky was darkening around them. Streetlights from the parking lot next to the courtyard bathed the area in a yellow glow.

"So do I." They reached the chairs and he rested his hands on the backs, ready to fold them up. Sabrina wondered why Lana had sent them both out to get the chairs when one of them could have done it easily.

"The kids love it, for sure. But I know the parents truly appreciate your sacrifice." She looked around at the cement buildings, thinking of the families who lived here. Homelessness was one of the worst things to happen to a parent. Not being able to provide even basic living arrangements for their child would be failing in a big way. Her chest tightened. And she was going to be one of those failures.

"Sacrifice? I just show up when Gavin tells me to," he said.

Sabrina rolled her eyes. "Giving up your evenings after a hard day's work is definitely a sacrifice." He was being modest. The man must work longer hours than she did. She wasn't naive enough to think a vice president sat around and shot rubber bands at the ceiling.

He paused, as if unsure what to say. "I'm afraid a hard day's work is new to me. I wasn't always the most committed employee. My father had a heart attack a few months ago and I've tried to be more responsible, easing the way for his return." He ran a hand through his hair, a gesture she'd come to recognize as something he did when he wasn't happy.

She thought that over for a moment. How would it be to have the sort of job where it didn't matter if you showed up to work or not? "I'm sorry to hear about your dad. He must be really proud of the way you've taken over while he's been gone."

There was an uncomfortable moment when Sabrina knew that she'd touched a nerve. Maybe his father wasn't the kind of parent who said what he felt, who let his kids know he was proud of the work they'd done.

Or maybe they weren't close. Whatever it was, Sabrina read his expression well enough to know that Jack's relationship with his dad wasn't as easy as it could be.

She cleared her throat. "My dad couldn't keep a job. He was an alcoholic who blamed everyone else for his problems. I try not to let his inability to be a good parent affect the way I live my life." She blew out a breath. "That sounds harsh, but—"

"I understand what you mean." To Sabrina's surprise, Jack was nodding. "I think I've been making a lot of decisions in reaction to my own father rather than doing what I needed to do."

"Is he someone you admire? Is he a good example?" She might be asking too many questions, but it had been so long since she'd had anybody to talk to.

He shook his head. "I love him. He's an honest man. But he's built a business empire at the cost of his family. I never remember him being present at the dinner table. He came home after we were in bed and was gone before we were awake. Christmas and Easter were two days he took off, but even then, he would be taking business calls all day."

"So, being chained to a desk is a terrible idea to you." She could see how he would never want to be that man. Jack's father sounded as absent as her own, even though one had worked all the time and the other couldn't keep a job.

"Exactly." He shrugged. "It's silly, but I didn't see how avoiding work was all about him. I thought it was about me and what I wanted out of life." She couldn't be sure, but his cheeks looked darker, as if he was embarrassed to admit it. Jack was a better man than a lot of the guys she knew from the old neighborhood. They considered an easy job a gift and would love to be in his position.

It seemed odd, out here in the fresh air, to see how quickly their conversation had turned serious. "I can't believe we're having a heart-to-heart right now about the fact our dads haven't given us enough attention," she said.

"Weird, isn't it?" He was smiling, but his tone was serious. "I feel like every time I talk to you, I understand myself a little better."

Sabrina felt her brows go up and couldn't think of a thing to say. It was probably the nicest compliment she'd ever been paid, and she was speechless.

"But I think I understand you a little better now. Remember when we first met, in the cafeteria?"

She nodded. She remembered how it had felt when he'd listened, really listened to her. It had been so long since anyone cared what she said that she'd forgotten what it felt like.

"I asked you how you knew that you wanted to be a mechanic. That was a stupid question and you told me so."

Sabrina shook her head, laughing. "I did no such thing."

"Oh, you did. In a nice way. But you did." He looked down at his hands. "Anyway, I asked you how you knew your purpose in life was to be a mechanic. Half of that question was right."

She looked up at him and couldn't seem to tear her gaze away. All that mattered was this man and what he was trying to say to her.

"Those girls are your purpose, aren't they?" He

jerked his head toward the cafeteria gym. "They're your reason for everything you do."

She nodded. "They deserve the best—a mom and a dad who love them and protect them —but that's not going to happen. I'm what they have now and I'm going to do the best I can." She looked up at the sky, blinking back sudden tears. "But I don't know what I'm doing. I only know that my parents failed at keeping me and my sister fed and safe. They never told us they loved us or listened to what we had to say. And now I'm moving my nieces into a homeless mission."

He reached out and touched her arm. "Life happens. It's not all about the material things. You're doing a great job, even if you have to live here for a while."

"Am I?" Her voice was fierce. "How do you know? Really, how can you tell?"

Instead of being offended by her tone, he stepped closer. "I can tell because I've known good parents, like Grant and Calista. Like you said, keeping them fed and safe are the basics, but I see how the girls look up to you. They want to be near you and they trust you. You're listening to them, building their confidence." He looked down at her, his blue eyes serious. She realized again how tall he was. He never seemed that way, never loomed over her or made her feel weak. That realization nudged against the hard wall she'd put up around her heart, the wall she used to keep people out and to help herself stay strong.

"Sometimes I get so scared." Her voice was barely a whisper. "I don't want to fail them. I feel like I already have."

He opened his arms at the same time she moved toward him. Resting his chin on her head, he whispered something into her hair. Sabrina squeezed her eyes closed, inhaling the fresh smell of his cologne, wishing she could stay there forever. She wasn't sure how it had happened, but here they were again, holding each other. She was tired of trying to figure it out and maybe, just for a moment, she could let it all go. She pushed away the visions of the workers last night, of Pancho's fear, of the boss's threats and the sickening knowledge that she had to do something to help the workers. Sighing against him, she felt his arms tighten around her, like a small circle of safety in an uncertain life.

He spoke, his deep voice a rumble against her ear. "I feel like the world is crazy, some days. Nothing makes sense. Then I see you and everything starts to fall into place."

She lifted her head, eyes wide. She had been thinking the same thing, but how could a man with Jack's education, job and family feel as if the world was out of control? Even more, how could he think she made it better?

He lowered his head, his gaze searching hers. Sabrina knew that she should put a hand to his chest and step back, but she didn't move away. The few seconds it took for his lips to reach hers seemed to last forever. He pressed his mouth to hers so softly, as if he didn't want to scare her. Sabrina leaned into him because being close to Jack seemed to be the only thing that mattered. She laid a hand against his chest and felt his heartbeat against her palm. A small part of her brain remembered they were standing in the mission courtyard, but they seemed to be the only two people in the whole city, in the whole world. As one kiss slid into another, it was just that thought that brought her back to reality.

The girls were inside with Lana and Gavin while

she was outside kissing their gorgeous soccer coach? She stumbled backward, her hand to her lips. Her face went hot with shame. All her self talk about keeping a level head had been for nothing.

Jack's expression went from soft wonder to concern in less time than it took for Sabrina to disentangle herself. "I'm sorry. I shouldn't have—"

"No, no, it was my fault." She rubbed her forehead and glanced around, wondering how many people had seen them. Surely there were families in those rooms, behind the windows that looked out over the courtyard. She felt one of his hands at her back and loved the warmth, the steadiness, but still moved away. It was a mistake to be here with him, when she couldn't offer him any kind of future.

"Sabrina, I should have asked you out before…" He waved a hand between them, as if at a loss for words. "I want to get to know you better. I love spending time with you. Maybe we could go out to dinner or something where we could talk."

Ask her out? Sabrina's heart twisted. It sounded wonderful, but there was one small problem. "Right, it's hard to have a conversation with all these kids around."

"Exactly." He smiled down at her, then seemed to realize she didn't look happy about the chance to spend time alone with him.

Sabrina sighed. Jack, as handsome and intelligent as he was, didn't really get it. "But you see, I don't have any life without those kids."

He looked as if he wanted to argue, but he said nothing.

She went on. "At least, I can't right now. If it was anything else, I could walk away for a little bit. But I can't afford to be distracted or to put anything else at the center of my life. I need to get permanent guardianship and now that I'm moving to this mission, it's all in jeopardy." She felt her throat tighten around the words but she swallowed hard. "I hope you understand."

"I do." He put his hands on either side of her face. "And I like you even more for it."

She looked up into his eyes and felt her resolve waver, just the tiniest amount. She wanted so much to be the kind of carefree girl who went on dinner dates or up on the mountain for the day, no cares in the world besides which outfit to wear. But that had never been her life and it never would be.

His gaze dropped to her lips and she wondered if he would kiss her again, but before she could decide how to react, he let his hands drop to his sides. "Let's get back inside before they send a search party." He grabbed the two chairs, folded them neatly and motioned for her to walk ahead of him to the door.

Sabrina nodded, feeling as if the earth was still shifting under her feet. She'd made a mistake kissing Jack, but had managed to set the record straight. She'd done what her parents never had, what Rosa never had, which was put her nieces first, because it was the right thing to do.

Then why did it feel so bad?

Oh, the irony.

Jack trudged back into the gym, a folded chair in each hand. He hadn't really considered that Sabrina would turn him down. She liked him, he could tell. From the very first day they'd met, he had felt her interest. It just had never occurred to him that Sabrina would think a date with him would be a distraction.

He liked girls, all girls, but he had never really wanted to be with someone the way he wanted to be with Sabrina. He glanced at her and tried not to sigh. Those dark brown eyes edged with thick lashes, the flawless tan skin, her full lips and high cheekbones. Those were all good things, but it was the bright spark of intelligence, the quick wit and the no-nonsense attitude that really got his attention. Add her iron resolve to make a home for her nieces and he was sunk. He didn't care if she was a homebody or hated the snow or loved cats instead of dogs. He wanted to know her better. And that didn't look as if it was going to happen anytime soon.

The gym was much quieter than when they'd left. The girls were racing up and down the blue line by the cafeteria entrance while Gavin and Lana chatted. He turned and jerked his head toward the supply closet. "It's still unlocked. Don't forget your toolbox."

Sabrina looked up, startled. "You're right. I almost walked out the door without it. That would have been bad if I got called out tonight."

"You do a lot of work in the evenings?"

She hesitated. "Not usually. I try not to, but every now and then…" Her voice trailed off and she turned to the supply closet, her shoulders tense. He could tell she didn't want to discuss it.

Jack walked the length of the cafeteria and set the folding chairs near the entrance. His whole body felt tired, as if he'd run miles. The day had started out with so much promise.

"Are you okay?" Gavin cocked his head and gave him a steady look. "You seem a bit down in the dumps."

"Nah." He shrugged and stuffed his hands in his pockets.

Lana and Gavin exchanged a look. "That's not our usual cheery Jack," Lana said. Her words were light, but there was a question in her voice.

"It's been a long day." He didn't elaborate but kept his gaze on Gabby and Kassey as they raced each other across the echoing space.

"Uh-oh." Gavin shook his head and started to laugh.

"What?" He tried to keep the irritation from leaking into his tone, but his best friend could really be annoying. Just because Gavin's life was going perfectly didn't mean that he could poke fun at Jack.

"I think someone got shot down." Lana said this very softly and rolled her wheelchair forward. She touched his arm. "It was bound to happen." She was teasing him, but there was honest sympathy in her eyes.

"I guess there's a first time for everything," Jack mumbled. He loved these two. Like Evie, they knew him too well. He watched Sabrina hoist the toolbox into her other hand as she crossed the gym toward her nieces. There was a sharp pain under his ribs at the thought of not being able to be any closer to her than he already was.

"Here I thought you were the pickiest person on the planet. I guess someone beat you at your own game," Gavin said.

"Not that you really need to know the details, but it's not about me." Jack grimaced as he realized what he'd said. All the girls used that line. Not with him, not ever, but he'd heard about it. "She would, but she has the girls to think about and…" The rest of the sentence went unfinished. Maybe she was only saying that so that she didn't hurt his feelings. The idea made his shoulders slump. If that was true, then it wouldn't ever be a good time, even when she had custody of her nieces. Then a swift memory of their kiss flashed through his mind and he knew Sabrina was telling the truth. She liked him; it was clear as day.

"You've got to admire her for that," Lana said, watching Sabrina herd the girls toward them. "She's got a lot on her plate right now. Too many parents put their kids last, and those wounds are hard to heal."

Jack nodded. He understood that Sabrina wanted to do the right thing. He just wished that her idea of doing the right thing included him. But she hardly knew him. A young woman who had fought her way out of a family ruined by addictions had to protect herself. For a moment, he wondered what it would have been like if Sabrina had been born into his kind of family wealthy parents, a good college education, the city at her feet. If they'd met in a different way, at a party or a dinner, they would be free to pursue a relationship without any strain.

"Come on, girls," Sabrina called to Gabby and Kassey. She was hungry and they'd be getting up early tomorrow morning. They ran over, giggling. Kassey's hair was coming out of her pigtails and Sabrina stopped to fix them.

They trooped out of the gym and into the lobby, and Gabby grabbed Sabrina's other hand.

"I can bring you home," Jack said. "It will be faster and you won't have to wait in the cold." He slipped on his brightly patterned ski jacket, zipping it in one swift movement. Tugging a striped cap over his head, he transformed from friendly soccer coach to ski geek in seconds. She had to admit the man was good-looking in anything, even crazy snowboarding gear.

"It's not that cold," Sabrina protested.

"*Tía,* can we go with Coach Jack? I hate the bus. It's smelly." Gabby leaned against her, small face turned up in supplication.

"You should go with Jack. I'd drive you, but I've got to meet Evie down at the paper." Gavin shrugged on his jacket.

"Nobody needs to drive us anywhere." Sabrina knew her voice was a little louder than normal, but they were making decisions without her. "We usually take the bus and we can tonight, no problem."

"Let Jack take you home. The girls can be in bed a lot sooner," Lana said, a note of finality in her voice. She turned to Gavin. "Evie's been working late for weeks now. She missed the last finance meeting."

Gavin nodded, his brown eyes somber. "She's been trying to get that story on the slave-labor rings past the lawyers for a long time. She's got a few more witnesses and personal accounts. It's just such an ugly topic, nobody wants to touch it."

Sabrina sucked in a breath. "What…what kind of story?" She couldn't have heard him right.

"Slave labor," Jack said. "Groups operate right here in the city, right under our noses. They hold people as hostages, work them night and day, move the operations more quickly than the city can track them."

Gavin seemed to misunderstand her expression and said, "Unbelievable, isn't it? But it's true. Evie has files and files on these people. It scares me to death sometimes, how far she's gotten in her investigation."

"That's my sister, always fighting for the truth. You can't stop her. It's worthless even to try," Jack said.

"Someone has to, it's true. I just wish the city would listen to her," Lana said. "We've had a few girls come through here who've been rescued from those places. They were just too scared to tell the police what they knew. Grant makes sure they have protection at all times. Finally, they start to feel safe. By the time we convinced them to talk, the groups were long gone."

Sabrina thought of the girl she'd seen in the kitchen the day she'd met Jack: frightened, nervous, barely able to function. Then she thought of Evie, with her dark hair and blue eyes, those matching dimples, just like her twin. She looked up, emotions in a tangle so tight that she could hardly breathe. These people were working against the slave-labor groups, doing everything they could, putting themselves in danger, even. And Sabrina had information they desperately needed. She took a deep breath, gathering her courage in both hands.

"Tía," Gabby said, tugging on her arm. "Can we go now? I'm hungry."

Sabrina looked down into her niece's face. Wide brown eyes implored Sabrina to get moving, innocence in every line of her face. She loved her nieces so much, more than she loved her own life. She reached out and smoothed back an errant strand of hair.

Sabrina cleared her throat. "Sure, *mija*. Let's go home."

She had to do something, help somehow. She had to think about it, find a way to get the information to Evie without jeopardizing her girls. As much as she wanted to keep her head down and try to stay safe, there were people suffering out there. And if someone like Evie was fighting the rings, how could Sabrina turn her back? Evie didn't know anyone who was in one of those rings, she could be sure of it, but Sabrina did. Pancho had been her friend once; his mother had fed her when she had nothing to eat.

Knowing that there were people working to free those poor workers gave Sabrina a shot of courage. She had an idea and she was going to do everything she could to bring the labor ring down.

Chapter Nine

"I'm parked out back," Jack said.

It was clear by Jack's expression that he thought she was a little wary of him, especially after that kiss. It wasn't that at all. She'd never felt so safe with anybody before. She wasn't worried he would try to change her mind or make her explain herself any more than she already had.

Her pride was the problem. She knew Jack was wealthy, probably lived in a gorgeous house out in Cherry Creek, the kind of place that could fit five families but usually had two people inside. When he saw their redbrick apartment building, he'd feel even more pity for them, and she hated the thought. The kiss they'd shared shone bright in her mind. She didn't want to tarnish it with shame.

Between having her pride hurt a bit more than it already was and giving him the impression she was afraid of him, it was no contest. Jack didn't deserve to think he'd done anything wrong. "Okay, we'll go with you, and thank you for the ride."

His expression lightened. "Not a problem."

They waved goodbye to Lana and Gavin and trooped out the door. Gabby was chattering about a book report she needed to finish and Kassey was quiet, gripping Sabrina's hand. The temperature had dropped and a cold chill swept off the mountains, right into the downtown area. Sabrina noted the groups of ragtag young people headed toward the mission to check in for the night. As they passed, one young man in drooping jeans and an oversize sweatshirt made loud kissing noises at her. His friends laughed raucously.

Sabrina felt Jack's steps falter and she spoke out of the corner of her mouth. "Don't stop. It's not a big deal."

He half turned, watching the men head down the sidewalk. Then he stopped altogether.

She felt alarm rise up in her. "No, Jack, it's really okay."

He glanced at her. "Just a minute." And then he was gone before she could say any more. He caught up with the group of teens in seconds.

Sabrina's heart jumped into her throat. First rule of the streets, don't confront those in power. And those teen boys might be homeless and uneducated, but they had the power here. There were four of them and only one Jack. He stood tall, but his hands were at his sides. She glanced at the girls, wondering whether to hurry them down the street or to stay. What if there was a fight?

The blood pounding in her ears made it almost impossible to hear, but she could see Jack speaking to the group. They had formed a semicircle around him, faces like stone. Jack put a hand out and laid it on the shoulder of the teen across from him. Sabrina flinched, expecting the teen to throw a punch in response. To her surprise, the boy nodded, glancing her way. Jack turned to the others, speaking too low for her to hear. They looked chastened.

Sabrina noticed how tight Kassey was clinging to her hand and she looked down, trying to be reassuring. "Everything is fine. We'll go in just a minute."

"But *Tía,* what if they fight?" Gabby hugged herself, her thick sweater doing nothing to keep her shivering at bay.

"I think it's going to be okay," she said, praying that what she'd said was true. But in the next moment, Jack had turned and was striding back toward them. The teens shambled off toward the mission, a little less cocky than before.

"Sorry about that," he said, jogging the last few feet to reach them. "Let's get you to the car and get warmed up."

"What did you say to them?" Gabby asked.

"Nothing much. Just reminding them of things they already knew." He didn't meet Sabrina's eyes.

She tucked her chin into the top of her sweater as they entered the parking lot. Any boy from her old neighborhood would have turned the situation into a posturing contest that probably would have ended in a fistfight. When it was over, they would have come back to reap the reward of the girl's eternal gratitude. But Jack didn't seem to want any applause for his actions. In fact, he wouldn't even share what he'd said. His calm discussion with the teens touched her heart in the same way his protection of her nieces had.

A car chirped to her right and she jumped.

"Sorry," Jack said. "Just hitting the unlock button."

He pointed toward a cream-colored SUV that sat near the front of the lot.

"Pretty car, Coach Jack!" Gabby cried. She rushed to it, ready to jump into the backseat.

"Wait," Sabrina called, hurrying to catch up. "Try to knock the dirt off your shoes. The parking lot is so muddy." Sabrina decided she'd better get the girls situated and then carefully sit with the toolbox on her lap. If she got grease in Jack's nice car, she'd never get over it.

"Don't worry about their shoes. I take this up to Wolf Mountain all the time. I've always got ski gear melting off in here and people with muddy boots." He opened the back door and helped Gabby and Kassey up. "Buckle in, you two."

"Let's put your box in the back," Jack said, moving toward the rear hatch. He swung it open with an easy movement.

"Good idea. There's usually some grease on it. Do you have a towel I can use? Something to protect the carpet?" Sabrina peeked into the space.

"Just set it in there. The carpet is black for a reason." He smiled down at her. "I'll strap it in with the cables."

"Strap it in?" Sabrina asked, hefting the box into the back.

He pointed to heavy-duty straps that ran from each end. "It's a safety thing. Keeps heavy items from flying toward the passengers in case of an accident."

"Great idea," she said, watching him tie down the box. She laughed a bit, shaking her head. "You're the perfect guy. Coaching kids, protecting young women, strapping down heavy items."

He tugged one more strap into place and glanced at her. He didn't smile. "I'm not perfect."

"Huh." Sabrina didn't know why she was pushing the issue, but his denial made irritation flare up inside of her. "So, having a high-powered job, athletic ability, a great sense of humor and being gorgeous isn't enough? We need something else? You must run in pretty competitive circles." The kind of circles where someone like Sabrina wouldn't even be hired as a secretary.

He slowly straightened up. Looking down at her, he spoke softly, "I like the sound of all that, especially the being-gorgeous part."

Her face went hot and she looked down at her feet. She noticed for the first time that there was a small hole in the toe of one of her tennis shoes. The closer he got, the more she wanted to push him away. She had been alone for so long that it was hard to let anyone into her life.

Reaching out, he lifted her chin with one warm finger. He met her gaze and his eyes were dark with emotion. "But we both know that perfection comes from above. I'm so far from perfect, Sabrina. I would trade all of the things you mentioned for being a better person."

They were inches apart, in the dark, the light from the SUV casting a glow around them. His hand was steady on her chin and for the merest second, his gaze dropped to her mouth.

Then he dropped his hand and stepped back, reaching for the SUV hatch. "Let's get you guys home."

She nodded, walking to the passenger side as he slammed the trunk closed. Why did she have to pick a fight every time they got close? Why couldn't she just make small talk like a normal person? Probably because she never had been very good at small talk. Making friends wasn't her area of expertise.

Pulling herself up into the passenger seat, she put on her seat belt. The interior of the car was dark, but the dashboard was dimly lit, as if it was already prepared for the driver. She glanced back at the girls, who were busy giggling and bouncing in their seats.

Jack angled into the driver's seat. "You'll have to give me directions," he said. His voice was light, but there was a tightness around his mouth.

Sabrina wished for the tenth time that she was a different girl. Someone who had the freedom to reach out to Jack and wipe the frown from his face.

"We're not too far from here," she said, forcing the words past the lump in her throat. She gave him quick directions and settled into the seat, wishing they were already home.

Jack could smell Sabrina's light perfume. Or maybe it was her shampoo. A weight had settled on his chest and he couldn't seem to shift it. That kiss in the courtyard had been completely unplanned, and yet he had to admit he'd been wanting to kiss her since they'd met. But she'd let him know that a relationship was not going to happen, not right now.

He turned onto the busy downtown road and headed west. He knew how to take rejection as well as any guy—not that he'd had that much practice with it. When she said she had too much on her plate, he understood completely. Sometimes the time just wasn't right for two people to start that tightrope of a romantic relationship. His brain understood all of that perfectly well; it was his heart that was having a hard time. Every time he looked into those dark brown eyes, he wanted to show her that he could be the man she needed.

Jack slowed for a red light, listening to the girls giggle in the backseat. Being a single parent was no laughing matter, and he admired her attitude of putting the girls first. It was true she really didn't need a man in the mix, but he sure wished she did. Jack grimaced inwardly. How petty to wish that Sabrina would let him rush in and play the knight in shining armor. Having a little chat with some trash-talking teens was one thing. Stepping in to support a whole family was another. She was doing a good job and he needed to keep his ego from getting in her way.

"Thank you for talking to those kids back there," she said, almost as if she read his mind.

Jack blinked. As the light turned green, he advanced slowly, watching the truck in front of him spew dark smoke from its rusted tailpipe. "I would have waited for a different moment, but I was thinking I probably wouldn't find them again." He chanced a glance at her. "I hope that didn't make you uncomfortable, I wanted to remind them that they have to follow the rules at the mission and those rules include showing respect. They probably didn't mean much by it, but there are women there who have suffered sexual assaults. That kind of behavior could make them feel very threatened."

"I agree. What is simply annoying to one person could cause a panic attack for someone else." Sabrina looked at her hands. "It was nice. I don't go in for the caveman type, but I appreciated what you did."

He almost choked. "Caveman type?"

Her lips tugged up. "You know, the kind of guy who rushes around looking for a chance to show his muscles and protect his woman."

"Ah." Jack nodded. "I know some of those, I guess."

His woman. Obviously she was just using a turn of phrase, but he couldn't help smiling.

They lapsed into silence and he was painfully aware of how close she was. There was a real difference between sitting at dinner, running around a gym and being in a small area like a front seat of a car. Minutes later, she pointed out a brick building perched on a darkened corner. It looked to be the sort of place where retirees might find themselves in if they didn't have enough to move to a warmer climate. The walkway was tidy, but the two small bushes at the front door seemed out of place, as if put there as an afterthought. The lack of underground parking told him more than the sort of drab surroundings. This wasn't an upscale neighborhood and this building wasn't the sort of place any of his friends might live, whether just out of college or not.

Sabrina reached for the handle of door. "Thank you for the ride. Just pop the trunk and I'll grab my tools."

He pulled up at the curb and put the car in Park. "It's late. I'll walk you to the door."

"No, really…" She started to protest but Jack was already out of the car.

Gabby and Kassey piled out of the back, still chattering, and ran for the front door. The dim light from the entryway wasn't very welcoming. Jack glanced up and down the street on the way around to the trunk. There wasn't a bus stop near. They must have to walk a few blocks even after catching the bus. He realized how much of a sacrifice she had made to allow them on the team.

At the rear of the car, he lifted out her toolbox. She reached for it and for a moment he wished she would just let him help. Why was it so hard to let him carry it, when it must weigh more than twenty pounds? He was taller, stronger and just wanted to help. But as he handed it over, he knew it was less about the weight of the toolbox and more about her independence. This was a woman who had worked hard for everything she had. She wasn't one to accept help when she was perfectly capable of handling it herself.

"Coach Jack, come on in and see my room," Kassey called. She was standing by the door and waving him forward with a huge grin.

"Thanks, Kassey, but I should let you guys get your homework done."

"I don't have any," Gabby said. "Do you, Kassey?"

"Nope, not me," the youngest girl said, her gap-toothed grin adding a little extra charm to her words.

"It's okay, you don't have to come up," Sabrina said, just as he knew she would. "Your car probably isn't usually parked on the street, right?"

He turned, frowning at the SUV. He hadn't thought about his car. He parked wherever he needed to, but she must think he always chose a secure garage. "I'm not worried about the car."

"Well," she said and then paused, as if unsure whether to finish her sentence. He almost spoke, telling her she didn't need to invite him up, that he didn't need any kind of payment for giving them a ride. She spoke before he could say what he was thinking. "Well, I'd love for you to come up and have some tea." She glanced up, unsure, as if he might be somehow offended at the invitation. "Or coffee, if that's what you like."

Jack was so surprised he just stared at her for a moment. They weren't going to date, but that didn't mean they couldn't be friends, he supposed. He loved talking to her, laughing with her. He thought of her when she wasn't around and looked forward to when he'd see her again. It might be a bad idea, but he couldn't bring himself to say no. "That would be nice."

A smile spread over her face and she said, "I can't promise it's clean. I was on the phone when we left this morning so there might be dishes left out and—"

"You're talking to a twenty-seven-year-old bachelor who lives alone. I don't think two small children and a grown woman can compete with the kind of clutter I leave around after a weekend up on the mountain." He held out his hand for the toolbox. She couldn't unlock the door and hold it at the same time. He was happy she didn't object, but just grinned at him and passed it over.

They walked into the small entryway, the worn carpet almost threadbare in places where the residents stopped to collect their mail from the wall of metal boxes. The smell of fresh paint was overwhelming and strips of painter's tape still clung to the corners of the ceiling.

"Coach Jack, I'll get out the cookies. I can reach them if I bring a chair into the kitchen and stretch way up high." Gabby was talking a mile a minute as she ran up the stairs, her pigtails flying out behind her. She disappeared around the turn of the stairwell and he could hear her footsteps heading up without a pause. Kassey was close behind, her short legs working hard to keep up.

"You're probably the most exciting thing to happen all month," Sabrina said.

"You don't have many visitors?"

They turned onto the second landing. Jack wondered for a moment if she lived at the very top. He didn't remember seeing an elevator. He was in good shape but he could feel the muscles in his hand complaining from the weight of the toolbox.

"Not really. I don't have much time after work. Evening is usually homework and bedtime. There's a girl upstairs who likes to hang out a bit and talk, but she's younger than I am. Most of her conversation is about fashion or what cute guy is her current crush."

"Sounds fascinating," he said. He shot her a look that said the opposite and she giggled. They reached the fourth landing and she reached for the door that opened to the hallway. Jack sent up a silent sigh of relief. His fingers were losing feeling.

"I'm not saying I want to debate politics or discuss current events, but I could really care less about the hottest brands."

"You don't need to." She turned with a confused expression and he went on, "You don't need to care about them. You're effortlessly beautiful."

Her cheeks went pink. "I wasn't fishing for compliments."

"I know." They headed down the hallway, Gabby and Kassey dancing with excitement in front of a brown door at the very end. "Maybe I'm prejudiced from living with Evie. She's always ignored fashion to the point of being hopelessly out of style. It drove our mother crazy. When Evie bought the paper, she decided to buy a nice wardrobe of office clothes."

"She looks lovely," Sabrina said.

"Well, she hired someone." Jack chuckled. "She said she didn't have time to fiddle with picking out clothes."

She laughed imagining Evie, so effortlessly put together on the outside and absolutely uninterested in her wardrobe on the inside. "Actually, I suppose I shouldn't be so quick to say I'm not interested in fashion. Maybe if I had the money and needed the clothes, it might actually be fun. I'm just not sure."

"Sort of how I've always felt about sports that don't include snow."

"But you coach soccer," she protested, laughing. She put the key in the lock of the door and opened it wide.

"Correction. I coach kids at the mission because Gavin asked me. The soccer is really secondary."

The girls ran through the door and split off in different directions. Sabrina looked around, her face going pink. "I'm sorry it's such a mess. I probably shouldn't have asked you up here."

"It looks like you're packing. Can I help at all?" The living room was small and littered with a few half-filled boxes. Bright red pillows were piled on the brown flowered couch. It was clean but shabby. He set the toolbox near the front door and took off his jacket. It was cool in the apartment.

Sabrina went to turn up the thermostat but didn't take off her sweater. "Thank you, but we don't have much to pack. Come on into the kitchen," she said.

The white walls should have made it seem bigger than it was, but the area was truly tiny. A square table sat in the middle, three battered chairs around it. Sabrina took a kettle from the stove and filled it with water.

"Have a seat," she said, motioning to the chairs. She seemed a little nervous, brushing her hair from her eyes and glancing at him.

Jack settled into a chair and stretched his legs out under the small table. The walls were bare except for a small photo of the girls with their arms around a young woman. Her hair was curlier than Sabrina's, but they shared the same heart-shaped face and large brown eyes.

"Is that your sister?"

She nodded without turning from where she stood at the stove, twisting the knob of the burner to high. "I thought it might help the girls if I kept a picture of their mom around."

"I thought you were trying to get permanent custody."

Sliding into the chair opposite him, she said, "Yes, but she'll always be their mom."

Jack thought of how he was struggling to make his way in the world without reacting to his own childhood and sighed. "It's strange how we never seem to get over the need for our parents' love. It's ingrained. It can't be explained away."

Leaning forward, her eyes wide with sincerity, she said, "Exactly. And if it can't be changed, I want them to have whatever peace they can. I don't want them to wonder. Growing up, I knew plenty of kids whose parents left them when they were too young to remember, and it seemed worse than what I went through. The not knowing was a constant torture."

Looking at the tiny scratched tabletop, Jack felt shame rise up in him. He had fought so hard to distance himself from his father. A lot of people wished they knew something, anything, about their parents.

"I drew you a picture," Gabby cried, running at full speed into the kitchen. She waved a sheet of paper at Jack's head.

"Thank you." Taking the sheet, he examined it

closely. Stick figures stood next to a house with a tri-angle roof. There was a medium figure with a pony-tail and a square box attached to one hand. This must be Sabrina. Two small figures held hands and sported matching triangle skirts and giant smiles. The next fig-ure was twice as tall and held both arms up, with small bumps at the biceps.

Jack started to laugh and then saw Gabby's eyes nar-row. He choked back his amusement and pointed to the tall figure. "This is me, right?"

"Of course. See how strong you are?"

"I do." He glanced up at Sabrina, expecting to see laughter dancing in her eyes. Instead, her face was bright pink and she jumped up to check the teakettle.

"I'm going to draw another," Gabby said and ran off to the bedroom.

There was an awkward pause and Sabrina cleared her throat. "Sorry about that."

"You don't like our family portrait?" He chuckled. "It's great. I love it."

She turned and shot him a look, as if she didn't quite believe him. "Guys usually run away when they see things like that."

He shrugged. "I don't know why they would. That kind of picture tells me how much she likes me and I'm honored." Sabrina didn't seem quite convinced. "When I was little, I drew a family portrait at school that had my mom, my dad, my sister, me and the garbage man. I thought he was the coolest man on the planet because he drove such a big truck. My parents were not amused, and it didn't get hung on the fridge, obviously."

She giggled. "Kassey loves the plumber. He comes

by pretty often and she says he's got better tools than I do."

As quickly as it had come, the awkwardness was gone. Jack watched her retrieve two mugs from the cabinet and let the muscles in his shoulders relax a bit. It had been a long day at work, with not much accomplished, but this moment was like a balm to his psyche.

The sound of a knock at the door interrupted his thoughts. Sabrina glanced at the little round clock on the wall and frowned. She seemed undecided whether to answer, but the visitor was insistent, knocking louder. "Mrs. Guzman is at her daughter's tonight. I wonder who that could be."

He got to his feet. "Maybe I should go."

"No, there's no reason to leave." Her gaze darted from side to side. "I'll just see who it is."

Jack watched her go into the living room and followed after a few seconds. Maybe she didn't feel comfortable telling him why, but it was obvious that she was afraid.

At the door was a middle-aged man, balding and with small, watery eyes. "I just wanted to make sure you were packing. You have to be out of here in forty-eight hours."

Jack could see Sabrina taking several large breaths. He moved closer, wondering if there was anything he could say to change Sabrina's predicament.

Mr. Snyder looked up and fixed him with a glare. "You brought in a boyfriend? There's an extra charge for another person."

"He's not my—"

"We're not—" They spoke at the same time.

"I don't care what you call it. If he stays the night,

you pay." Mr. Snyder's lips turned up in a sneer. "Unless it's a one-night stand."

Jack strode forward and put a hand on Sabrina's shoulder. He could feel her shaking, but again he wasn't sure if it was fear or anger. "Would you take a check from me?"

"No, Jack," Sabrina whirled around, expression furious. "I really don't need you to pay my rent."

"That's right, you don't. You need to start packing." Mr. Snyder shuffled his feet and waited. Jack noticed his shoes were so highly shined he could see reflections in them.

"You've delivered your notice and now you need to leave," she said to Mr. Snyder.

"So does he," he said, pointing behind her at Jack.

She pulled in a deep breath and looked up at him. She wasn't angry. She just looked so very tired. His heart squeezed. Someone who worked as hard as Sabrina deserved a bit of respect. Jack nodded. It wasn't worth fighting the manager over. The situation was ugly enough as it was.

Jack didn't mind being booted from the apartment. He could see how this was going to end and he knew Sabrina had to stand her ground. Fury was rising in his chest and he fought it down. Getting into an argument with this man wouldn't help her at all. He grabbed his coat from the couch and slipped it on.

Mr. Snyder grunted and stayed where he was. Jack had the feeling the guy wasn't going to leave until he did.

"I'll go say goodbye to the girls." He walked the few feet to the open doorway that spilled the sounds of little-girl laughter. Peeking inside, he wasn't surprised to see the floor covered with paper and pens and crayons. "I've got to run, but I'll see you two at practice."

"Already?" Gabby jumped up and wrapped her arms around his waist.

Jack knew the mission had rules about hugging kids, especially without their parent present. He had to walk a fine line sometimes between being a coach and a family friend. He patted her on the shoulder and slowly stepped back. "Don't forget to bring your jerseys, okay?"

"We won't," Kassey assured him. Her little mouth was turned down at the corners, but there wasn't anything he could do about it.

As he came back into the living room, Mr. Snyder was tapping one foot impatiently. If Jack had never heard him speak, he would have figured the guy for a pushy, obnoxious little man. Add in the vicious attitude and Jack had the very lowest opinion of Sabrina's building manager.

He touched her arm gently. "I'll see you later."

She looked up, her mouth tight. "Yeah. And sorry about…" She glanced toward the kitchen, where the kettle was letting off a low whistle.

"Not your fault," he said. He walked to the door and looked Mr. Snyder in the eyes. "I'm not sure what the problem is here, but I sure hope you have good reason to be evicting Sabrina. There are laws about this sort of thing."

The manager tried to hold his gaze but blinked and looked down at his shoes, shuffling to the side to let him pass. Jack stepped through the doorway, keeping his hands in his pockets. He was tempted to grab Mr. Snyder's shirtfront and shake some sense into the man. Harassing someone like Sabrina made no sense at all.

She was stable, quiet and kept the place clean. But he knew bullies had their own reasons for what they did.

As he walked down the hallway, he couldn't help noting the stained ceiling and the faint smell of cooking grease. He wanted, more than anything, to turn around, walk back through that door and tell Sabrina that he could find them a wonderful apartment in a great part of town, with a manager who respected her the way she deserved. He forced himself to keep moving, step after step, toward the stairs. Sabrina was not the type of woman to take charity. He was very sure of what she'd say to any kind of offer like that. And he admired her for it, even while it frustrated him. She was moving to the Mission, and he wished he could just make everything better. But she was determined not to accept any help.

Pushing open the door to the stairs, he blew out a breath and started jogging down the first of four flights to the bottom. It would have been wonderful to sit and drink tea with her, to listen to that soft accent, to watch her dark eyes flash with emotion, but he knew it was better to go now. They were friends, by her request, but he had a feeling it was going to be very hard to tell his heart to stay firmly on that line in the sand.

Chapter Ten

"Bob, those production figures for the past six months don't make any sense. The costs are going up and our contract with Packaging International should have protected the company from any price changes." Jack stood in the doorway of Bob Barrows's office and crossed his arms over his chest. The time for gentle persuasion was past. He had finally cornered the elusive production manager and he was going to get some answers.

"I'll have to check into it," Barrows said. He reached for a five-inch-thick stack of paper to his right. The man's glasses were smudged and his hair seemed greasy, but his suit was obviously very well made. Jack knew about nice clothing, thanks to his mother's constant guidance, so he could spot a custom-made suit at twenty yards.

"Have you spoken to Packaging International? Have you asked why they're charging us twice as much as when we first signed the contract for the vitamin powders?"

"I have. All they can tell me is that costs doubled

on their end due to city tax levies." Barrows wiped his forehead with a handkerchief.

Jack frowned. Had Denver passed new ordinances for businesses? He mentally kicked himself for being oblivious for so long. He usually didn't notice anything unless it affected his snowboarding and now he was reaping the harvest of his ignorance.

He took off his glasses and wiped his face. Jack wondered if Barrows was ill. He looked nervous and shaky. "When is your father coming back to work? I heard rumors that it would be soon."

"Within the next few weeks. I'll let you know when we've got a firm date." Jack wished he knew for sure. When he'd dropped by the house early this morning, his father was out playing golf. It was good to see him doing something other than work, but it also meant he was well enough to return. Jack wanted to get these figures straightened out before that day.

Riding the elevator back up to the top floor, Jack let his mind wander back to last night. Sabrina's quiet anger at the building manager had stayed in his memory. It wasn't just her control, it was the feeling that she knew that if she protested too much, she would only come out on the losing end. The only time Jack had ever known that feeling was in one situation, and that was so long ago that he had almost forgotten it.

The elevator buttons blinked on and off as he rose higher and higher. In high school he had tried to explain that his dreams had not included a future in the family business. His father had made it very clear that if Jack didn't follow his advice, there would be no college, no home, no contact whatsoever.

A light ding sounded and the silver doors slid open.

He walked out into the lushly decorated lobby. Sleek black chairs were arranged artfully under a red-and-white abstract painting. Jack opened the glass door to his office and stood for a moment, looking out at Wolf Mountain in the distance. The sun gleamed brightly on the snowcapped peak and he closed his eyes, imagining how it would be up there on such a perfect spring day. He could almost feel the wind in his hair and smell the pine forest.

He sighed and opened his eyes, looking down at the stack of papers in his hands. Sabrina had held her anger in check because she needed to give her nieces a home. She was acting in their best interests. Jack had agreed to what his father had planned for him because he was too afraid to go out into the world alone. Looking back, it was probably for the best, but the more he learned about Sabrina's life, the more he realized something.

There had been a time when he had been sure that if he put off his dream of opening a snowboarding clinic up on the mountain, he would eventually be a bitter old man. He imagined himself still sitting in the fancy glass office, fifteen stories above the streets of Denver. But that wasn't the reality.

He sat behind the polished mahogany desk and flipped over the first page of the report. If he had learned anything these past few weeks, it was that time was precious. Getting to know Sabrina had taught him responsibility, but she had also given him courage. For the first time in a long while, he had a clear vision for his future, and it was here at Colorado Supplements.

"Hurry up, girls," Sabrina called. They had five minutes to make the bus and get to the mission for soccer practice. The thought of seeing Jack had kept her from complete despair. He and the girls were the only bright spots in a world that was growing darker every day. After what had happened the last time she'd seen the slave laborers, she was barely keeping her sanity. Haunted by the memory of leaving the girls and unable to see a way to report on the slave-labor group, her nighttime hours were filled with nightmares. Along with packing all their belongings for the mission, Sabrina didn't know if her anxiety could go any higher.

It seemed to take ages to get the girls down the stairs and out the door. Just as they stepped into the chilly morning air, she remembered she needed to get cash to pay Mrs. Guzman for watching the girls last week. They hurried across the street and Sabrina put her card into the ATM. She punched in the PIN and sighed a little as she entered the amount. She wished she didn't have to work during the evening, but being available at all hours was a boost to her income. The machine dinged and Sabrina squinted at the screen. Not able to complete the action? What did that mean? Maybe the ATM was out of money. That was possible, wasn't it? Sabrina's mouth was suddenly dry. She poked the option for a balance slip and in the few seconds it took the machine to spit it out, Sabrina's heart had dropped into her shoes. She took the piece of paper with shaking fingers and stared at the amount. A negative amount was printed clearly; she couldn't deny it.

"What's wrong, *Tía?*" Kassey stood up on tiptoe to read the paper, but Sabrina moved it away.

"Nothing. Let's go catch that bus." She turned and started down the sidewalk.

"But what about the money?" Gabby asked, trotting after her.

"I'll get it later." There would be no money later. Sabrina sucked in deep breaths as they hurried to the bus stop. A terrible suspicion started to grow in her mind. She was incredibly careful with her accounts since she didn't have the leisure to lose track. There was only one time she had not been in perfect control of her funds. It had been just weeks ago—the conversation with Rosa.

Her sister had never called back after that day and Sabrina had forced herself to not focus any energy on being angry. Rosa had had her cell phone bill paid and hopefully would get a job to support herself now that she was done with the internet boyfriend. He had never wanted Rosa's kids, never had time for anything except a good time. She hadn't called to talk to Gabby and Kassey, and Sabrina let it go. But now it seemed that giving her sister her debit card information might have hurt them all more than she could have known.

The bus pulled to the stop as they arrived, and she shepherded the girls up the steps. Her mind was whirling and she felt as if she couldn't catch her breath. She pulled out her phone and tapped out a quick text. Rosa never responded to texts and never picked up the phone when Sabrina called. Sabrina had to tell Rosa what her betrayal meant. Bile rose in her throat as she wrote the words and pushed Send.

Sabrina tucked the phone into her pocket and reached out to the girls. She hugged them tight against her, fighting back tears. What looked like a very temporary move to the mission until she could save up for another apartment was now looking as if it might be something a lot more permanent. She had failed them. As hard as she tried, she had still failed to be the family they deserved.

Sabrina tried to focus on the kids milling around the gym but her mind kept wandering: the bank, the missing money, her sister's betrayal, the slave-labor ring, Pancho, Jack's offer to help them out. She was so tired, so utterly defeated that it was all she could do to keep moving. *Lord, after everything I've done, this is how it turns out? Are You punishing me for leaving them alone that night?* She'd been wrong, but it had been the lesser of two evils. Bringing the girls under the gaze of the labor boss would be an act of insanity.

Finally the practice was over and she waited for the girls at the door as they helped Gavin and Jack put the chairs back into place. Even though she'd worked up a sweat, Sabrina felt chilly. The shock of seeing her bank balance had cast a shadow over her entire life. But she couldn't just lie down and give up, no matter how much she wanted to, because there were two little girls who needed her.

Gabby and Kassey seemed to have accepted the idea of moving into the mission, but the thought still sent anxiety rushing through her veins. She had always told them everything would be okay, and now she was going to move them into a homeless shelter? She felt sick with fear. All the memories of her childhood came rushing back. So many times her father had gotten a job and then lost it weeks later. So many times her mother had cried quietly in the kitchen because there was no food to feed her kids. Sabrina had promised herself she'd never rely on anyone the way her mother had. She'd always work hard and take care of herself. But it hadn't been enough.

"*Tia,* our first game is this weekend," Kassey shouted as she ran toward her.

"I know, sweetie." Sabrina had written it on the calendar weeks ago, before Rosa had called, before everything had gone wrong.

"Coach Jack is bringing cupcakes for everybody and we're going to win," Gabby said, perfectly confident. "We're going to win because we work hard and try our best."

Sabrina felt her throat close up in sorrow. A child's faith was a beautiful thing except that her confidence was no guarantee. She didn't want to see Gabby disappointed, but couldn't bring herself to tell her it might not work out.

Jack came up behind them and said, "It's not all about winning. It's about working as a team." He smiled down at the girls and gave Gabby a wink.

She giggled and raced through the door into the lobby.

"Do you really believe that?" Sabrina couldn't keep the bitterness from her voice. She didn't know why she was picking a fight. "I'd think the coach should care about winning just a little bit."

He slung an arm around her shoulder and kissed her temple. The move was so easy, so natural that Sabrina couldn't help the silly smile that crept across her face.

"If you think kissing me is an answer, then you're wrong," she grumbled, warming on the inside at his touch. Not to mention the fact that they were supposed to be just friends.

"No, the kiss was just because." He smiled down at

her, dimples in sharp relief. "And about the winning, I meant what I said. I know a lot about sports and teams. Even world-class snowboarders have a team—you just don't see them. No one succeeds all alone. We all need each other."

She frowned, searching for some example to prove him wrong. "What about bakers? What about gourmet-cupcake makers? You have a team in your kitchen?"

"I didn't grind the flour or process the sugar. I didn't churn the butter or get the eggs out from under the chickens." He still had his arm around her shoulders as they reached the lobby. Lana glanced up and her lips twitched at the sight of them.

"Huh. If you want to get technical about it..." She shrugged. He was right, in a way.

"If you think of someone who is successful without a team, no matter how distant, you let me know." He let his arm fall to his side and walked toward the desk. "I can bring you guys home."

"No, that's not necessary. You don't have to give us a ride every time there's a practice. We're perfectly fine taking the bus." Sabrina frowned.

There was a pause and she looked up to see an expression on Jack's face that made her giggle. His exaggerated expression of frustration, eyes looking upward, was so unlike him.

"It's a ride home, not a marriage proposal." His tone was light but he shook his head. "Do you ever let anybody help you?"

Her smile slipped a bit. "I do. Mrs. Guzman upstairs watches the girls when I have to go out." Except for the time there was no one and she had to leave them alone. Her stomach clenched. If she had a team, if she had

let herself make friends, then her girls wouldn't have
been alone in the middle of the night. "Sorry, you're
right," she said, sighing. It was just a ride, even though
her heart was growing more and more attached to him
each day. She looked up at this man who had done so
much for them, even as she pushed him away again and
again. "Thank you."

"You're welcome," he said. He seemed half surprised, half grateful they weren't going to argue about
it anymore. It was a standard response, but the tone of
his voice made it seem as if they were the only two people in the lobby. The sound of the girls' chatter faded
away and she felt heat rising to her cheeks. She couldn't
fathom how Jack could still be interested in her after
all of this. The idea that he really liked her, for who she
was, was hard to believe.

Lana's gaze flitted to where the girls waited and
back. Sabrina had told them she wanted to tell the girls
herself, at home, when they were alone. "Call if you
need anything at all. We have a lot of people here who
have gone through this, and who also work with kids
in crisis."

Sabrina was thankful that Gabby and Kassey seemed
like they were taking the move in stride. "I will."

Minutes later they pulled up at the apartment and
Jack put the SUV in Park. "Let me walk you to the
door," he said. He saw Sabrina open her mouth as if to
argue, then she nodded.

"Thanks." It was one word, but it seemed as if she
had finally gotten the idea of accepting a little help,
at least.

Jack angled out and opened the back door for the

girls. They scooted out, giggling. "Hurry up, *princesas*," he said. "This carriage is going to turn into a pumpkin any minute."

They rushed to the door, eyes bright with laughter. Sabrina hesitated, half turned toward the door. "Thanks for the ride."

He grinned. "See, not so hard. Just a ride—"

"Not a proposal," she finished for him. Even though her eyes had dark smudges underneath, when Sabrina laughed it was as if she was lit from the inside. Jack could just stare at her for hours.

"You'd know it when it happens. You wouldn't have to guess," he said, chuckling. Then his own words echoed back in his head and he wanted to slap himself. He had always been so good with women, never tipping his hand, never showing too much of himself. But with Sabrina he just couldn't keep from putting every feeling he had out on the table. The moment he opened his mouth, his thoughts came rushing out, for better or for worse.

Would she walk away? A few kisses had scared her into a friends-only talk. Two mentions of marriage proposals in an hour might have burned the bridge on their relationship.

"Noted," she said lightly. Her cheeks had turned pink and for once she didn't seem to be edging away from him. There had been some sort of shift in her, in the way she looked at him.

"See you at practice," he said, not able to think of anything else. He wanted to stand on the sidewalk all night and just stay in her presence, but they were adults with responsibilities. He had a pile of papers to fight through and she had an apartment to pack.

"See you," she said. But she didn't move away.

He felt his eyes widen as she stepped closer, tilting up her face. She pressed a kiss, so very softly, on his cheek. Then she was gone, walking quickly to the front door while he stood rooted to the spot.

Sabrina had kissed him. She had bridged that space between them and kissed him. Jack watched them go through the door and she turned as she closed it, catching his eye. Her smile was a bit embarrassed but was mostly just happy. Very happy.

He slid behind the wheel, unable to keep a grin from spreading over his face. Something was definitely different. He put the car in gear and pulled away from the curb, a feeling of utter contentment wrapped around him. Just as he reached the first light, he sucked in a breath, finally understanding what had changed.

Maybe Sabrina, who never let anyone help, was making a real choice to find her team. She wasn't going to fight the people who wanted to support her, insisting on doing it all herself. Being forced into the homeless shelter might have brought that change about, but Jack knew enough truly stubborn people to know that wasn't it. She was taking to heart what he'd said, and nothing could have made him happier.

Sure, the kiss was great, too. Just the memory of it made him grin. But Sabrina was choosing to trust other people, maybe even for the first time. Nothing was better than that.

Gabby leaned into Sabrina's side and buried her face into her shoulder. They sat in a row on the couch, the three of them. "*Tía,* why do we have to leave? Why can't we stay?"

Sabrina had already explained it as best she could, but she knew how hard it was to understand money as a small child. "Because, sweetie, we just don't have the money Mr. Snyder needs."

"I have two dollars from Easter," Kassey piped up. She looked so hopeful that Sabrina blinked back tears.

"We need more than that, *mija*." She hugged them both to her, feeling how small they were, how fragile they felt under her hands. These two deserved so much more than a homeless mission.

"But I thought you had enough. You said there was money to pay him and now there isn't. Did you lose it somewhere? Can we go look for it?" Gabby asked.

Sabrina closed her eyes for a moment. If she wanted to vent her anger, she would tell the girls exactly who had stolen their money. Rosa had texted back one line to her message earlier: Sorry. I'll make it up to you. It was so inadequate, so ridiculous to think an apology would make it all better, or that it could be made up in any way.

She let out a long breath. Telling the girls where the money had gone wouldn't hurt Rosa, it would hurt them. She was their mother, for good or for bad, forever. Any criticism reflected on the girls because they were her children. It didn't do anyone any good to share the details.

"I made a mistake. That's all," she said. It was the truth. She shouldn't have trusted Rosa.

"But we're sticking together, as we always have. You're my sweet girls and I love you." She placed a kiss on each of their heads.

"We'll move to the mission tomorrow. You like it there, right?"

They nodded, expressions full of fear.

"Then it will be fine. We'll stay there until we can find a new place. And maybe the next place will have an elevator."

Gabby perked up at this. "I love elevators!"

"Well, that's something to look for, right?" She heard the false cheer in her voice and hated it. "Let's eat some dinner and get ready for bed. It's been a long day."

The girls straggled to the kitchen and sat down, quieter than normal. Sabrina grabbed some bread and cheese, toasting them in the oven for a quick meal. They ate in silence and she tried not to worry. Kids were adaptable. As long as they were surrounded by love, they would thrive.

Sabrina forced herself to swallow the toast. All of these words were just to make herself feel better. She knew as well as any adult who'd suffered through a terrible childhood that upheaval left scars. Even though she would have some protection from the slave-labor bosses now, this wasn't the way she had wanted it to happen. They would all try their best, but it was going to be hard, maybe the hardest thing she'd ever done, to shepherd these beautiful little girls through the nightmare of homelessness.

It had only been a day since he'd seen Sabrina, but Jack felt as if it had been weeks. He wanted to call her, offer to come and help them pack, but he resisted. She knew where he was. And he would see her tomorrow at practice. Part of him was irritated that she hadn't asked for help, but another part knew that was who Sabrina was. Even though she was slowly learning to trust, it didn't mean she was going to call him every morning and ask for favors. He let out a breath and tried to focus on the pile of messages by his phone. There was a lot of work to do, whether he wanted to be here behind the desk or not.

A light knock on the door brought his head up with a snap. Employees were slowly learning that he could be approached when there was a problem, but it was still rare to have a visitor.

Jack opened his office door and felt his jaw drop. "Dad?"

The man standing there was as familiar as the back of his hand, except for the smile on his face. His dad wasn't known as a smiler. "Surprise," he said, opening his arms in a here-I-am motion.

"Come on in," Jack said. Then he paused. "Unless you want to go talk in your office."

"No, no, this is fine." He settled himself in one of the wing chairs across from Jack's desk and crossed his legs. His face was thinner and more lined than just a few months ago, but a heart attack had that effect on a man. His gray hair was just as thick but was freshly trimmed. Overall he looked good and Jack was glad to see him so relaxed.

"So, I hear everything is running smoothly." His father leveled a gaze at him.

Jack paused, confused. "Who told you that? I mean, things are running as well as we could hope, but there are a few issues I think need to be addressed."

"Bob Barrows called a few days ago. He seemed to think you were taking a little too much interest in his department. He assured me he's handling production the same way he always has, competently." Eyes narrowing, he frowned. "I'm glad you're taking a renewed interest in your position here at the company. It's certainly been a long time coming. But we don't need to micromanage the department heads. They've earned my respect, and I except you to show them the same."

Jack choked back a retort. His father was right. He hadn't paid much attention to this job for years. It probably looked as though he was meddling in departments on a whim.

"I'm glad you're here. I have something to tell you. I asked all the departments for a two-month audit, just to make sure nothing had changed after you…" Jack paused. His father didn't like to look weak, and that included saying what had taken him out of the office and put him in the hospital. "Your health scare. Most of the departments had no trouble bringing me a quick update. Production was different, though. I had to hound the man just to get a stack of printouts."

Jack pushed the pile of papers to the front of the desk, but his father didn't make any move to look at them.

"I went over the numbers three times. I contacted Packaging International. The bills here are from three months ago and the company says they haven't had any orders from us since December."

His father frowned. "That's impossible. We're shipping product around the world, and the warehouse is stocked. I just visited this morning and there were boxes to the roof."

Jack rubbed his forehead. "I know, I went out there, too. At least the vitamin supplements and the powders are all in stock. But if Packaging International isn't bottling and labeling the product, who is? And where is all this money going? Barrows has submitted payment requests as if we're still working with this company, we have the product, but the company says they haven't seen any orders for months."

"There's some simple explanation. What does Bob say?"

"He says I must have gotten ahold of the wrong person over at Packaging International."

"And who was it?" His father looked almost relieved, as if Jack would have made one phone call and left it at that.

"I first called their customer service, then was connected to someone in client relations. Finally I just drove out there to talk to them yesterday." Jack had wasted an entire afternoon driving out of the city and tracking down a company that insisted they weren't clients, even though accounts payable at Colorado Supplements thought they were. "There's nothing from us in their factory, no orders running, no labels, boxes, product. Nothing."

His father sat back in his chair and was silent. "What does that mean?"

"I don't know." Jack had gone over and over it and had come no closer to a solution. "What I can tell you is that Bob Barrows is at the center of whatever it is, and he knows I'm asking too many questions. I knew this before, but the fact that he called to talk to you just confirms that. I was going to come over and tell you about it today, but here you are."

His father had never been one to accept Jack's opinion out of hand, but he nodded. "I think you're right. Whatever's going on, it can't be good. At the very best, we're being scammed and losing money. At the worst, we're losing product and money."

Jack could think of a few worse things than losing

money and product: there could be illegal activities involved, such as drug smuggling or kickbacks to city officials. "The first order of business is to get some real account statements from the production department. We need to bring in other managers and see if we can find these missing figures."

"And if Bob already knows you suspect him, he'll be working hard to cover his tracks."

"Exactly." They sat in silence for a moment, feeling the weight of the issue bearing down on them.

"Are you back now, for good?" Jack was afraid to think his father was going to jump right into this mess after a heart attack.

"Only mornings, for now. The doctor said less stress and more exercise." He stood up. "I'll be in my office until noon."

His father paused at the door and looked back. "You've done really well here, Jack. I know you haven't always been happy to work here, but thank you for holding the place together while I was gone."

And with that he left, closing the door behind him.

Jack sat there, motionless. His father had never thanked him like that before. Probably because he'd never worked hard enough to earn any thanks. The heart attack had been a blow to their family in a lot of ways, but it also seemed to have brought them closer together. Jack had stepped up and taken responsibility, and his father had learned to appreciate the people around him a little more.

He had Sabrina to thank for all of it. He wished there was something he could do for her, but she wouldn't let him. She was proud, and he loved that about her, but it would be so much easier if she would just accept his help.

Jack's head went up with a snap. Maybe she wouldn't accept his help, but she might take assistance from someone else. Even better, if it wasn't a person at all.

A smile flooded his face. As soon as he could, he was going to ask Grant to help with his plan. Lord willing, there might just be a way to get Sabrina into an apartment after all.

He glanced down at the sheets of numbers. Now if he could only figure out what sort of scam Bob Barrows was pulling on them, he would feel as though he'd really earned that thanks. His dream of a snowboarding clinic still hovered at the corners of his imagination, but for now his job was to expose the lies that threatened Colorado Supplements.

Chapter Eleven

Sabrina fell into bed, her eyes closed before she even hit the pillow. Moving their furniture upstairs into Mrs. Guzman's apartment had been exhausting, even with Mrs. Guzman's nephew helping her. The day had been draining in all ways. Taking the first step to move into mission was one of the hardest things she'd ever done, but she was at peace with it now. It was for the best. The girls would be safe, she would be able to get to her usual jobs and they would be with friends. Tonight was their last night in this apartment, and then they would be official residents of the Downtown Denver Mission.

Jack's face flashed through her mind and her lips turned up. That kiss had taken him totally by surprise. She wished she had a picture of his expression, something to look at when she felt down. Stepping toward him, and not away, was one more brave thing that she had done that day. What he'd said about teams had really touched her. Everybody had supporters, even if they were distant. As a mom to her nieces, she didn't want to be alone. She wanted to have a safety net. She'd always figured it was best to go it alone, to keep from being hurt, but isolating herself had actually caused more problems.

Jack had spoken truth and it had been hard for her to accept it, but she was going to try, one step at a time, to let other people help her. It didn't mean she wouldn't be independent, although at this point, she had lost almost all her independence anyway.

You'd know it when it happens. You wouldn't have to guess. His words about a proposal made her smile in the darkness. Something she loved about Jack was how utterly guileless he was. She knew too many people who weighed every word, who never made a move in friendship or in business unless it benefited them. Jack was the sort of person who chose his friends without any other thought than if he liked them. She could imagine a proposal of his would never be a sneaky surprise— any woman who was blessed to get a proposal from Jack would see it coming a mile away, no guessing required. It wouldn't come out of the blue, for sure. He probably couldn't even keep his Christmas presents a secret.

A knock at the door made the smile drop from her lips. Not again. Not now. Sabrina slipped from the bed and crept to the front door. She listened at the crack, afraid to look through the peephole. If it was Mrs. Guzman needing help, she would have called. Unless her phone wasn't working.

She stood there, unsure of what to do next, when a voice called from the other side. "Sabrina, open up!"

Pancho, and he sounded as panicked as before. Her mind whirled and she took a deep breath. Did she have the courage to put her plan in motion? After the last time she'd gone with him, she'd sat at the kitchen table until dawn, forcing herself to find a way out of this mess. Only one idea had occurred to her, but it involved going there, into the heart of the slave-labor ring, one last time.

She unbolted the door and slid back the chain. Pancho's face was tense and his eyes were red. He said nothing, just waited for her to speak.

"I need to call Mrs. Guzman," she said and reached for the phone. His eyes narrowed and for a moment she wondered if he was afraid she would call the police on him. That had occurred to her, but then she'd remembered Mrs. Olmos, Pancho's mother. The organized-crime leaders would hurt her and her children, and she had nothing to do with any of this. Mrs. Olmos had saved Sabrina and Rosa when they were little. There was no way she could put her in harm's way now.

As soon as Mrs. Guzman answered and was headed down, Sabrina hurried to dress. Now that she had a plan, she felt almost eerily calm. *Help me shut them down. Protect me, Lord.*

Minutes later they were out the door, Mrs. Guzman tucked up on the couch. Sabrina loved that old woman, loved how she was ready to be present when needed. Jack would call her part of Sabrina's team. It occurred to her that she wasn't part of Mrs. Guzman's team. She never helped out, or came when needed. As she followed Pancho down the stairs, she started to see her life as very empty, not only of friends, but of times when she could have supported the people around her. There must have been times Mrs. Guzman needed help, but had called someone else.

As she slid into Pancho's car, her toolbox on her knees, Sabrina felt tears prick at the corners of her eyes. She had tried to be independent, to take care of herself, but she had also refused to be present for other people. This wasn't what she'd ever imagined her life would be, shut off and cold, fighting to take care of her family. She had only herself to blame. But no longer. She was ready to help, to put herself out there the way people did for each other, trusting that it was the right thing to do.

A brick warehouse loomed in the darkness and Sabrina fought back a shudder. They had driven in silence, interrupted every so often by Pancho's racking cough. He sounded too sick to be out in the cold night air, too sick to be out of bed, but she didn't comment about it. He had no choice, just like her now.

The door swung open to reveal a completely different warehouse, but the occupants were the same. The workers looked exhausted, maybe a little dirtier. The machine sat idle in the middle of the room, surrounded by boxes of labels. Against the wall were ceiling-high stacks of boxes, probably full of the product.

"Get it fixed," the boss grunted at her. He parked himself on a chair in the corner and crossed his arms over his belly.

Sabrina didn't respond, unsure if her voice would be strong enough. She wasn't afraid now, not fearing for her life the same way she had the first time or sick with fear over her girls alone in the apartment. No, she had a plan and she was going to do her best not to arouse the man's suspicion.

As she pulled on her coveralls and bent over her toolbox, Sabrina prayed harder than she'd prayed in her life. So many people depended on Sabrina being able to play the part of the frightened girl mechanic one last time. Unplugging the cord, she didn't even glance at the workers leaning against each other. Her heart ached for them, but she didn't meet their eyes. She leaned into the machine, adjusting the pressure pads underneath the labels, her fingers reaching deep into the rollers for the bits of paper that had jammed it.

Finally she had it cleaned and ready to run. She turned to the box, reaching for a stack of labels, when the boss barked at her from his seat on the chair.

"No touching," the boss yelled.

Sabrina jerked her hand back and looked to Pancho. He shrugged and called to a man sitting on the concrete. "Test it," the boss ordered.

She stood back as the machine roared to life. In seconds packets of powder were flowing smoothly down the belt, receiving labels and being deposited into a box. The workers sprang into action without being told. Closing up her toolbox, Sabrina waited for Pancho to get permission to take her home.

The boss walked over and stood silently in front of her. She looked up, her mouth dry. Did he know? Had he seen what she'd done?

"Remember, I know where you live." The boss fixed her with a glare that made her skin crawl. His eyes were murky and yellowed, as if he was suffering from some sort of kidney issue.

She dropped her gaze to the ground and nodded. If she could just get out and get back home, then she would have a chance to bring this whole place down.

"Take her home," the boss said to Pancho and went to the door, waiting to throw the bolt behind them.

Getting into Pancho's car, Sabrina fought not to look behind her at the warehouse. She was so close to making it back home, where she could examine what she'd pulled from the machine that was now tucked safely into the pocket of her coveralls. The torn label wrenched from the very heart of the machine could mean the difference between life and death to so many people, including her nieces.

Minutes later Sabrina sat at her kitchen table, the small light over the kitchen sink the only illumination. She pulled the label from her pocket and smoothed it out with shaking fingers. At first her brain couldn't make sense of the words. Then the truth of it fell against her heart with a power that knocked the breath from her lungs.

Colorado Supplements was written in bold letters over the top of the label. Jack's company was the one that had hired these men.

"If there's anything I can do, please let me know," Grant said. The director was standing in the doorway to Sabrina's new home. It was only a room, with a bathroom down the hall and no kitchen, but it was their home now.

"I will." She glanced at the girls as they unfolded their blankets and made up the thin mattresses on the metal bunk bed. They were giggling and whispering to each other as usual, but she had seen the sadness in their eyes as they left their apartment. It was the only home they'd ever known and now it was gone.

"When is the hearing? Lana said you might need someone to give a character reference."

"In three weeks." Even saying the words made her stomach flip-flop. It would have been difficult to stand in front of the judge before, knowing her future with Gabby and Kassey was on the line. But now it made her positively sick with nerves. "I have to declare any changes in residence or employment, so I've already sent in a form to the local office. They should receive it by then."

Grant cleared his throat. "I'm not saying that moving to a homeless shelter is a good thing, obviously, but we have many stable families come through here. It feels awful, I know. But try to remember that it's not the end of the world."

Sabrina nodded. She couldn't imagine how the director, married to a CEO and with a darling little boy, could understand how she felt right then.

As if reading her mind, he said, "You probably think I've only seen this from one side, but I was homeless for several years in high school. I lived on the streets before finally coming to the mission."

Her head snapped up in surprise. Grant, polished and handsome, had been a street kid?

"The director helped me get my GED and apply for college scholarships." He glanced around the room. "Staying here is a way to keep from going any further down and a step up. It's not the bottom. I've seen the bottom."

Her eyes burned with sudden tears. She spent so much time judging people that she hardly knew who was standing right in front of her.

"I didn't know that. I just wish…" She looked to the girls, now pulling books from their backpacks and putting them in neat piles on a small table. Her throat closed around the words.

Grant put a hand on her shoulder. "I know," he said softly. "And that makes a big difference. Some parents don't care, and those kids carry that forever."

She looked up at him, thinking back to what Lana

had said the other night, about wounds that were hard to heal. Sabrina's father had loved his beer more than his children, and she was still fighting through those issues. She wanted to make a stable home without depending on anyone else, while Rosa could never seem to stay in one spot or with one person. They were both stuck dealing with having an alcoholic parent. For a long time, Sabrina had thought it was only Rosa who had the issues.

"Thank you," she said and tried to put everything she couldn't find words for into those two words.

Grant nodded, looking as if he understood what she meant to say, and closed the door softly behind him as he left.

Sabrina took the label out of her purse and stared at it. Of all the things that had happened lately, this one item was the one that had knocked her world from its axis. She would see Jack at practice tomorrow, but before then, she had a phone call to make to the local police department.

Jack knocked lightly on the doorframe to the mission director's office. "Grant, are you busy?"

"Not at all, just working on paperwork. Come on in," he said, waving Jack into the office.

He sat in the chair and took a deep breath. "I need your help."

Grant's brows lowered. "I'll do what I can, you know that. Tell me what you need."

"I need you to…" Now that he was here, he wasn't sure how to describe his plan. "I need you to lie." He hurried on at the look on Grant's face. "No, wait. That's not quite right. I just don't know how to explain, or where to start."

Grant came around the desk and leaned against the front. "How about you start at the beginning."

Jack nodded. "Sabrina needs an apartment."

"She sure does," Grant said. He looked even more confused.

"She's got a hearing in family court in three weeks and I think they're not going to be happy about her being in a homeless shelter. I've asked her if she'll let me pay for an apartment, but she won't even listen to me."

Grant crossed his arms over his chest. "Hmm."

"I know this is putting you in an awkward position," Jack said quickly. "I thought if we did this just right, though, there wouldn't be any outright lying. It would just be sort of omitting the whole truth. And it's for a good cause." Grant's expression made Jack's stomach drop into his shoes. He didn't look receptive to the idea at all. "You have to admit that letting me pay for an apartment will get her a better chance at keeping her nieces."

"Oh, I agree with that part. And I have no problem keeping the donor anonymous. We've had grants available to residents before and the donor didn't want to be named. It's not so unusual."

"Then you'll do it?" Hope rose in him and he started to smile.

"I'm not sure, Jack." Grant shook his head.

"But why?"

"Sabrina could get very angry if she finds out that she told you not to pay for an apartment, and you did anyway."

Jack blinked. He hadn't thought that Grant would be afraid of Sabrina, but he could see how a grown man might be wary of her. She was a loving, tender person, but she also had a core of steel under the surface. "Maybe she won't blame you. Maybe she'll lay all the blame on me," he said.

"That's what I'm afraid of," Grant said. He sighed. "I don't want to pry into your business, but I've seen the way Sabrina looks at you. Are you sure you want to risk losing her over this?"

Jack nodded and spoke slowly. "I do. I've thought it over. If it gives her any kind of chance to keep her nieces, I'll do what it takes to make that happen. Even if it means she…" His voice dropped away. She what? Broke up with him? They weren't dating, not really. The idea of losing her was like a hot knife in his ribs, but he was resolved to do what he could to ensure she won permanent guardianship.

"As long as you understand that this could have major relationship fallout," Grant said. His eyes were shadowed with concern, but he held out his hand. "You're a good man, Jack. One of the very best. And I'm proud to call you a friend."

Jack swallowed hard and shook Grant's hand. "Thank you. Now, let's get this plan in motion."

Chapter Twelve

"Mr. Thorne, there's an officer here to see you," Tina said. Her forehead was furrowed and her red lips were compressed in a thin line. Jack looked up, surprised— not at her words, which hadn't really sunk in, but by the fact that his secretary was becoming more and more comfortable knocking on his door. For years she'd just taken messages and passed them on to other people who were more interested in doing his job.

"Show him in," he said and moved a pile of papers to the side.

A tall man in a Denver City Police uniform strode in and Jack stood to greet him.

"Daniel Daley," he said, shaking hands. His gray hair was thinning in the front, but he had the lean body of a runner, even though he must have been close to fifty.

"Have a seat. How can I help you?" Jack asked. His thoughts went to Sabrina and her move to the mission and her custody hearing. But surely they didn't send out officers for character statements. He couldn't be here because of Sabrina…unless there was something she was hiding. Her face flashed before his eyes. That night she signed the papers to allow her to coach, she had seemed afraid, as if there was a dark secret in her past.

"I'm sorry to disturb you. I wanted to speak to your father, but he seems to be on a leave of absence."

"He's been at home, recovering from a heart attack," Jack said. "But he's been working half days."

The officer tilted his head. "So he hasn't been able to keep a close watch on his company while recovering, but you've been running things around here."

Jack paused. As far as he knew, he hadn't done anything illegal. He wasn't the most experienced vice president in the history of business, but it was nothing to call the cops over. "Can you tell me what this is about?"

"This morning the city raided a warehouse on the east side." Daley paused and watched Jack's face.

He nodded. "Okay." He couldn't imagine why the man was sitting in his office.

"We found a small but lucrative slave-labor ring."

Jack sat back with a thump, his mouth dropping open. Evie had worked so hard for so long to bust the rings she knew were operating right under the noses of the city.

"You're familiar with this group?" Daley leaned forward, eyes narrowed.

"My sister has been investigating them for years." Jack felt a smile spread over his face. She must be thrilled, ecstatic. He couldn't wait to congratulate her. Then a thought occurred to him that wiped the joy from the moment.

"Officer, was anyone hurt? Is that why you're here? I told her not to go poking around by herself." Jack felt bile rise in his throat. If his twin had been hurt, he would be lost, without an anchor. Sweat broke out on his forehead.

"No. No one was hurt." The cop was still watching him intently. "But we did find a connection there between the slave ring and Colorado Supplements."

"I'm not surprised. Evie has been trying to make contact with anyone connected to the rings. She probably..." His voice trailed away as the officer's words sank in. *Colorado Supplements*. Not *The Chronicle*. "Excuse me?"

"We found evidence that this company has been using illegal labor to produce or manufacture the product sold." Daley's hands were resting on his thighs, perfectly relaxed, but he was watching Jack's face without blinking.

"Evidence?" He could only manage the one word through his shock.

"Labels, vitamin powder, bottles of pills waiting to be packaged and shipped."

Jack sat for several seconds, stunned. He had known there was a problem but at the worst he'd thought Bob Barrows was embezzling funds. He'd been sure that an internal audit would reveal a kickback program with another vendor, or a false front used to bill *Colorado Supplements*.

"Do you deny knowing anything about this?" The officer was calm and polite, but Jack could hear the edge to his voice. He could imagine how angry the man felt, seeing the results of that kind of abuse. Evie had told him stories that gave him insomnia and now it seemed as if his own company was the culprit.

"No," he said. Then as Daley's eyes widened, Jack held up a hand. "I mean, I don't deny knowing about the slave-labor rings. As I said, my sister has been trying to run a story on them for years. She's very active in social programs that combat human trafficking, here and internationally."

After a long pause, he shook his head. "I should have known," he whispered. He sat forward, feeling as if the air had been sucked from his lungs. His own voice sounded weak to his ears. The company his father had worked so hard to build, the company he should have been dedicating his time and energy to, was implicated in something illegal...and it was so obvious he must have been blind to miss it.

Sabrina lay on the narrow bed and rested her forearm across her eyes. In a few hours she and the girls would head down to soccer practice. Gabby and Kassey were playing quietly with a board game. Sabrina knew how much they loved practice, and of course she was also coaching, but if there had been any way to get out of going tonight, she would have taken it. She squeezed her eyes shut tight and tried to relax.

Calling the police this morning with the location of the warehouse and the tip about Colorado Supplements had been one of the hardest things she'd ever had to do. It was the right thing, though.

Fifteen slaves were saved from their lives with the criminals, and although Pancho was surely in jail, he wouldn't be blamed for the raid. Sabrina's call to the police had focused on Colorado Supplements, not on anyone from the neighborhood. As far as the gang leaders knew, it was someone associated with the business side, not any of the people she knew. Pancho had been in fear for his life, just as she was, so there may have been a way he could have received a lighter sentence. All she knew was that Mrs. Olmos should be safe. She prayed she would be. Sabrina and the girls had nothing to fear now that they were at the shelter.

But in a few hours, she would see Jack face-to-face. She would have to explain her role in what had happened to his company. The idea made her stomach twist in on itself.

There was a light knock on the door and she sat up in the bed, heart pounding.

"Sabrina, can I talk to you for a moment?" Grant asked, poking his head inside.

"Of course," she said. She stood up, arms wrapped around herself.

"There's a grant available for single parents who need to find an apartment, and I thought of you."

"A...what?" It was so far from what she had been expecting that Sabrina had trouble understanding his words.

"A grant to help single parents move into apartments." Grant glanced at the girls. "It's perfect for you and your nieces."

"But aren't there people ahead of us on the list?" Sabrina couldn't imagine that they would be up for a special program like that after only two days in the mission.

"The donor asked that it be reserved for specific cases. Single parents, young kids, and it pays for first, last and down payments. The parent would need to have full-time employment and be drug and alcohol free."

Sabrina stared at him. She didn't want to take any charity, but here she was, homeless. The time for sticking to her pride was over. "When could we move?"

Grant reached into his pocket and handed her a

folded piece of paper. "There's a nice place over on Seventh Street, by the river, a few miles from the girls' school. It's near the bus line, so you could still get to your jobs. Also, it's only fifteen minutes from here, so we'd be thrilled if you could keep coaching."

Sabrina read the paper several times. The apartment manager had already agreed to rent to her, with Grant as cosigner. "Are you sure you should sign for this? You can't possibly do this for all the residents. You could get into real financial trouble."

He chuckled. "You're very right. And this is the only time I ever have, or ever will. This donor would like to remain anonymous. Since I know you, I'll cosign, and then after six months my name will drop off the lease."

She blinked back sudden tears. Grant said he knew her, acted as if they were friends. She felt he trusted her more than she trusted anyone. Except maybe Jack.

He went on. "I know you don't want to take money from anyone, but think of the hearing in three weeks. This answers their concerns about the girls being in a mission."

"Yes, that's true." Her voice was barely more than a whisper. "And you won't tell me who donated the money?"

"Nope." He was smiling now, seeing the gratitude in her eyes.

She swiped at her tears and then took a breath. "Okay. Tell me when."

"Tomorrow afternoon. Jose and a few of the men from the offices can retrieve your furniture from your friend's apartment."

"Wow." She was stunned. Happy, excited, relieved. So many emotions she could hardly define them all.

"That's what I said," he agreed. "We'll see you all down at practice in a few minutes?"

"Right." She was still staring at the apartment paper. "Gavin and Jack are probably already there."

"Probably just Gavin." Grant frowned, his hand on the doorknob. "I think there's been some trouble over at Jack's company today. We may not see him for a while."

Her heart leaped into her throat. "Why?"

"I don't know all the details. I should wait for him to explain it. The police are investigating a link between a slave-labor ring and their production department."

Sabrina could hardly ask the question, but it had been the only thing she could think of all day. She knew the answer, or at least she thought she did. But she still had to ask. "So it had nothing to do with him?"

"No. I can say that with confidence. Evie has been trying to run a story on these groups for years, but the lawyers for the paper always shut it down, fearing they'd be sued. Her sources were people who were too afraid to speak up, afraid their families would be targeted."

She knew exactly what he meant. Pancho had wanted out but didn't want his mother or siblings to suffer the consequences.

Grant said, "I guess someone managed to get the attention of the city, and they moved in before the labor ring knew what was happening. Jack said it looked really bad for Colorado Supplements." He shot her a glance. "But don't worry. Jack is a good man and he'll come out on top."

She nodded, her gaze on her shoes. He was definitely a good man. She just hoped he didn't suffer for what someone else had done, and what she had had to do. What would Jack say when he found out she was the one who had brought his company to the attention of the police?

"I'll let you guys get ready for practice." He stepped through the doorway. "And congratulations on the new apartment."

Sabrina collapsed onto the bed. She was so overwhelmed it was hard for her to think clearly. A new apartment meant the custody hearing might go better than she had feared. She had no idea how she was going to survive until the court appointment. All she could do was try to keep busy. And pray.

Jack jogged to the front door of the mission, the spring air cool against his skin. He swung the door open and grinned at the sight of Gavin, Grant, Lana and Jose crowded around the desk. He'd missed this place, missed these people. It wasn't the same when he skipped practice, even if it was because he was dealing with the scandal that had rocked his company. It was amazing how quickly life could change. Only days ago he'd been given terrible news, but then life had swung around once more, leaving him to shake his head at the way God could mend the broken places.

"Is it a party? Are there cookies?"

Grant chuckled and came to shake his hand. "Good to see you back. We missed you here."

"Lana got a mysterious delivery of cupcakes from Tasty Temptations, that bakery on Eighth Street," Jose said.

"Hmm. I can't imagine who would think the mission needed more cupcakes but didn't have time to make any." Jack leaned over the counter. "Are there any dark chocolate with orange essence left?"

"Ha! I told you so," Lana said, lifting up the tray for him to see.

"Hey, Sabrina, would you like a cupcake?" Jose called out.

Jack turned, his heart rate doubling. Sabrina was coming through the door, as beautiful as ever. Gabby and Kassey ran ahead, laughing. "Cupcakes? We want one!"

"If it's all right with your aunt," Lana said.

"Sure," Sabrina said. She shot a glance at Jack and then looked away. He'd thought she would look happy and relieved but she looked, if anything, unhappier than when he'd seen her last week.

The girls each grabbed a cupcake and then wandered toward the gym.

"How's the new apartment?" Grant asked.

"Perfect. We love it." Her voice was soft, as if she was afraid of speaking too loudly.

Jack cleared his throat. He had thought she would say hi to him at least. The last time they'd been together, she'd kissed him. It had seemed, for once, that she was learning to accept help and to trust other people.

She looked up at him and her smile faltered. "Could I talk to you for a minute before practice, Jack?"

"Sure," he said and waited for her to go on. It must have dawned on Grant at the same time as on him that she meant privately. There was a pause, and suddenly Grant announced, "I'll be in my office. Jose, didn't you have papers to fill out?"

"What?" Jose frowned at him. "Oh, right. Papers." He followed Grant to the door that led to the offices.

"I need to…" Lana searched around the desk. "…check the lights outside. I think they were about to burn out last night." She wheeled her way toward the door, her hands moving in swift strokes.

Jack snorted. "That was weird." He expected Sabrina to laugh, but her face was as far from laughter as he'd ever seen it. She looked panicked and tearful. "Sabrina, what's wrong?"

"I called the police on Colorado Supplements," she blurted.

For a moment, the words made no sense. He shook his head, struggling to catch up.

"A friend of mine from the neighborhood, Pancho, came to my door one night. He needed a mechanic. He brought me out to a warehouse in the middle of the industrial district." She hauled in a breath, her brown eyes wide.

"You...saw the slave laborers?"

"I worked for them." She swallowed hard.

His mouth opened but no words came out.

"Three times I went to fix machinery for them. They knew where I lived, they knew the girls were with me. Once..." She paused, wiping tears from her cheeks. "Once there was no one to watch them, so I had to choose between bringing them or leaving them alone in the apartment."

Horror squeezed his chest. He couldn't bear to ask the question.

"I left them alone. In the middle of the night, I left them." She hauled in a breath, forcing herself to keep speaking. "I knew I had to find some way to report the slave-labor group without letting them know who it was. So, the next time, I looked at who was hiring them."

Now her shoulders were shaking with sobs. "I'm

so sorry, Jack. It was the only way I could see to save them and my girls."

He reached out and gripped her shoulders. He wanted to crush her to him, to hold her tight until all the fear and horror was gone. But he dipped his head and looked her in the eyes. "Sabrina, you are the bravest person I know."

"You're not angry?"

He shook his head, fighting back a laugh. It all had come full circle. "You saved me, Sabrina."

"But how? I've ruined your family's company. Everything your dad worked for is now tangled up in the slave-labor ring."

"No, it's not." He wanted so badly to kiss her mouth, her eyes, the tears on her cheeks, but he needed to explain how everything had worked out. "Remember when we first met?"

"Of course," she said. "In the cafeteria. You held the hood of the chopper for me."

"And we talked."

She nodded. A smile touched her lips. "I forgot what it was like to talk to a friend."

"That day changed my life. I realized I needed to work harder at my job before I quit to follow my own dreams. I had earned a salary at that company and done the very least possible. I'm not proud to admit that at all. I was focused on my plan for a snowboarding clinic, and my father's company wasn't part of that, except for how much money I could earn for showing up."

"But you've been working so hard." She seemed confused.

"I have. And part of that was asking for audits from all the departments." He was grinning now. "Sabrina, you may have called the police on Colorado Supplements, but you didn't ruin us. I had already seen something was wrong with those numbers, and when the police came, I handed over all that work. It was work I'd done because of you."

"So…" She started to smile, tears still fresh on her face. "Your company will be okay?"

"I think so. They've arrested the man who was running it from the inside. Meanwhile, my father won't be charged for something he didn't do."

Sabrina threw herself into his arms and he held her tight, pressing his cheek against her hair. "I'm so glad," she said, her voice muffled by his shirt.

"I am, too." He had never admired any woman so much, had never been so completely captured. "I love you," he said, letting his emotions guide him.

She leaned back, looking straight into his eyes. Her expression was full of wonder, and happiness shone from her. "But why?" she whispered.

He let out a bark of laughter. "Why? That's not what you're supposed to say."

Her cheeks flushed pink and she ducked her head. "I'm just surprised that someone like you could love someone like me. I'm a single mom. I have grease under my nails and no social life."

Leaning down, he kissed her lightly on the lips. "I love everything, everything about you, but we're going to have to fix that part about the social life. I want to take you out to dinner, bring you and the girls up on the mountain, spend hours talking with you."

Her eyes filled with tears again. "Are you sure? We're so different. I mean, just a week ago I was homeless, and you help run a company."

"We're not so different in the ways that matter. We're the same in faith, and values. I love how you'd do anything to protect your girls." He paused, hoping now was the right time, praying his words didn't cause a rift between them. If they were going to be together, he didn't want any secrets between them. "I need to tell you something about that grant you got from the mission, though."

"What is it?" she asked, surprise marking her words.

"I'm the donor."

She moved back, eyes fixed on his face. "You mean, you set up that grant for single parents?"

"No, I mean I set it up for you. Just for you." Alarm stirred in his chest. He could see her getting angrier and angrier.

"Even though I told you I didn't want you to," she whispered.

"Yes." Dread filled him. Grant had been right after all. Sabrina was furious that he had gone against her wishes. "I thought you might be angry, but I hoped you would understand why I did it."

"You lied to me and went behind my back to get your way." She jerked out of his arms and stalked away.

"Sabrina, wait," he called, but she kept walking. "I did it for the girls."

Seconds later she had gone back into the gym, the door swinging closed behind her. Jack stood there, feeling as if all the happiness had leached out of the world. He had done the right thing, and if he had to, he would do it all again. But he had lost Sabrina's love and respect in the process. His throat tightened at the thought of life without her. He had become so used to her smile, her thoughtful words, her presence. He couldn't imag-

ine how he was going to go on, living day to day in a
world that didn't promise at least a hint of her laughter.

He shoved his hands in his pockets. There had been
one shining moment when he had felt her lips against
his and he'd been able to tell her how much he loved
her. And then the moment was gone forever.

Chapter Thirteen

"Miss Martinez, I see you have provided for your nieces in the absence of their mother." The judge glanced down at a sheet of paper and frowned through the bifocals on the end of his nose. "You had a recent stay in a homeless shelter?"

Sabrina cleared her throat. Her palms were sweaty and her heart was pounding so hard she could barely hear. "Yes, sir."

He looked up, his piercing blue eyes fixed on her face. "How did that happen?"

"I wasn't able to pay the rent, sir." She paused. What other reason would a person have for living at a homeless shelter?

He flipped through several sheets of paper. "You make enough money to pay the rent, unless these forms are inaccurate."

Sabrina hesitated. She could either say the numbers she'd provided were wrong, or she could explain. She couldn't bring herself to describe how Rosa had stolen the money right out of her account. No matter what Rosa had done, she was still her sister. She might never see her again, but she didn't want to brand her a thief in front of the whole world. "I loaned money to someone and she didn't pay it back." That was true, in a way.

He leaned forward. "You loaned money that you needed to pay the rent?"

"The apartment manager also raised the rent, including a new deposit and cleaning fee." She couldn't keep the anger from her voice. She hated that she was sitting here, trying to explain how she'd become homeless. "I already knew we had to move. I was trying to find a place for us, and then..."

The judge glanced at the clerk to his right. "There have been several complaints about Park Plaza," the judge said as if that explained everything.

Sabrina felt her heart rise. Maybe the stint at the homeless shelter wasn't such a negative after all.

"Miss Martinez, I have to tell you that this sort of scenario doesn't look good for an application of permanent custody, even if the mother is out of the picture."

Please, Lord, don't let him deny me custody. All Sabrina had left was prayer. She had nothing left to give as an explanation.

"But your strong work history, your character references from the director of the mission, the statements from the girls' teachers all say you are doing a good job caring for your nieces. Also, your ability to get into an apartment again so quickly tells me that you're determined to succeed in life."

She nodded, hoping against hope.

"I'm awarding you permanent custody of Kassandra Martinez and Gabriella Martinez." He looked up, a smile spreading over his face. "Congratulations, Miss Martinez, on your new family."

"Thank you, sir," she said, her voice choked with tears. She felt as if an enormous weight lifted from her shoulders and she couldn't help beaming back at him. "Thank you so much."

Minutes later, she was walking out of the courtroom, her heart pounding in her chest. She couldn't wait to go home and tell the girls the good news. They were a family, forever.

She paused on the courthouse steps. The judge had made it seem as if getting into the new apartment had been a major factor in his decision. Sabrina felt a stab of pain at the thought of the person who had made that happen, and she couldn't fight back the image of Jack's face. She missed him, more than she had ever missed anyone in her life. It had been almost two weeks since she'd seen him at the mission. She had brought the girls for practice but told Gavin she couldn't help coach anymore. She had made it sound as if moving into the apartment and doing extra jobs was taking all her time, but it was really because she didn't think she could face Jack. Even though he had gone behind her back, she still yearned for him. Her heart ached with how much she wanted to hear his voice, to touch his skin.

She swiped tears from her eyes. Every time she wanted to weep over him, she reminded herself that she had trusted him and he had lied to her. Even worse, he'd made her a charity case. He had ignored everything she'd said and gone against her wishes. Those weren't the actions of an honorable man.

Or were they? The judge's words echoed in her head. *Your ability to get into an apartment again so quickly.* Jack had known she might be angry, but he had paid for the apartment anyway. He'd said he'd done it for the girls.

Sabrina felt the dawning of a new feeling, one of regret. She had focused on how Jack had gone over her head and how her pride had been hurt, but really the focus should have been on the girls. She hauled in a shaky breath. He had acted in their best interests, just as a parent would, no matter the consequences.

She started down the steps, her heart pounding in her chest. She needed to tell the girls the good news, and then she was going to find Jack. A few words might not be able to heal the rift between them, but she needed to thank him, at the very least, for what he had done.

"I've waited all day for practice, *Tía*." Gabby skipped alongside Sabrina, her pigtails bouncing.

"I've waited all week," Kassey said. Her eyes were wide with excitement. "I can't wait for our game on Saturday. We're going to win, I just know it."

"I'm sure you do," Sabrina said. She was barely listening, her heart thumping painfully in her chest. Jack would be here and she wasn't sure if they were even friends anymore.

"Hi, girls," Lana called out as they walked in. "Go on into the gym. I need to talk to your aunt for a second."

The girls ran on ahead through the double doors and Sabrina watched Lana roll her chair across the lobby.

"Hey, congratulations on getting custody yesterday."

Sabrina beamed. "Thanks. It went really well. I was worried about explaining how I ended up here, but it all worked out."

"It must have helped that you have an apartment now." Lana cocked her head.

Sabrina knew that the secretary wasn't just congratulating her. "You heard about our fight."

"You mean, how you got upset that Jack took care of you guys?"

Sabrina shook her head. "You don't understand. I trusted him," she choked out.

"He betrayed you?" Lana folded her arms across her chest. "He's in love with someone else? He never liked you at all? He lied about who he is and what kind of man he wants to be?"

"Well, no." Sabrina bit her lip and stared up at the old wooden cross on the mission lobby wall. "But he lied."

"Sort of. We all did. Most of the staff knew about it and said nothing."

Sabrina stared down at Lana, shocked at how calmly the middle-aged woman admitted to what they had done. "Why?"

"Because the girls needed to be with you. Because judges don't look fondly on women who lose their apartments." Lana leaned forward, her eyes narrowed. "Sabrina, no matter how good you are to those girls, you are going to do them a real injustice if you don't learn to accept help."

She clenched her jaw, refusing to accept the truth of Lana's words. She had always managed to keep them afloat by herself. She had provided for them and loved them and… A small voice whispered in her heart, *and she had failed them.* Doing everything herself had made them homeless.

"Maybe you're right," she whispered.

"No maybe about it. And that man in there—" Lana pointed back through double doors into the gym "—wants to love you."

She felt her face go hot. "Maybe if he loved me, then he wouldn't have lied to me."

Lana sighed and rolled her eyes to the sky. "Do you know anything about men?"

Her spine stiffened and she wanted to walk away. "So I've never been in love—" *Until now.* Her heart finished the sentence for her. She struggled to go on. "But that doesn't mean I can't understand men."

"A man like Jack, someone who is faithful and honorable, he wants to provide. He wants to keep you safe. If he has to hide his identity so you'll accept his money in order to save your girls, then he'll do it. Even if he knows you'll be angry with him later."

Sabrina looked back toward the gym. "He said that?"

"That you would be angry? Sure he did. But he put himself out there so that you could be somewhere safe."

She stared at her feet. "But I just walked away from him. He was trying to explain and I walked away. I haven't talked to him since."

"And that's the end of the story?" Lana started to laugh. "Sabrina, I can't tell you how many times I've had to say I was sorry. Hundreds. Thousands. Don't make this the end if you don't want it to be."

She nodded, then impulsively leaned down and wrapped her arms around Lana. She could smell vanilla and coffee as Lana squeezed her back.

"I won't," she whispered.

Jack saw Sabrina enter the gym and his heart beat double time. He had braced himself for a cold greeting, or maybe none at all, but she walked straight to him. Her expression was fragile, gaze searching his.

He held up a finger in a just-a-second gesture and

jogged to the supply closet. Reaching inside, he retrieved a manila envelope and turned to see she was almost to him.

"I heard the good news," he said.

She nodded, a smile crossing her face for the first time. "The judge gave me permanent custody."

"Congratulations on your new family," he said, then paused. "I mean, congratulations on being legally declared a family."

Her eyes sparkled with laughter. "Exactly right. We've always been a family."

"I brought you a present in honor of the occasion," he said.

She frowned down at it. "You didn't have to."

"I know. Just open it."

She slipped her finger under the flap and peeked inside. Tugging out the fragile paper, she held it up to the light. "Is this a map of...Denver?"

"Denver, circa 1925. I saw it in a shop a few days ago and thought you might like it for your collection." His stomach twisted as he watched her face. Sure, he'd said it was a present to celebrate gaining custody, but it also was a gesture from a man to the woman he loved. How she responded would tell him everything he needed to know about his chances with her and the future they might have.

"Thank you," she said. But her voice wasn't exactly thrilled. Jack's heart dropped into his shoes. She was being polite and accepted his gift, but she obviously had no desire to start up where they had left off. Wherever that was. They hadn't been dating, hadn't even gone out to dinner, but she had stolen his heart.

"Jack, I need to say something." Her shoulders were

back and her chin was up. Jack knew that she was steeling herself for something difficult. His stomach dropped. He'd known there was a chance he would lose Sabrina over paying for the apartment, but he hadn't known, until this moment, how much it would hurt to hear the words.

"Go ahead," he said. "But before you do, I want to say that I'm glad for having known you." She looked up, eyes widening. His throat was tight, but he went on. "You've made me a better man, Sabrina."

She nodded. And took a deep breath. The sounds of the gym faded around them and Jack readied himself to hear the woman he loved say there was no chance for them.

Sabrina searched for the words she'd practiced all morning. She'd come here to say something important, and nothing would stop her. Not the way Jack smiled down at her, not the way he smelled, not the way she felt her heart tugging her toward him in a way she couldn't fight any longer.

His gift was just one more way that proved Jack knew her better than anyone else. He knew her dreams and her hopes, her fears and her strengths. To other people, it was just an old map. To her, it said everything about the sort of man he was, considerate and kind, tender and thoughtful. He deserved complete honesty, and it was time to tell him what was in her heart.

"I'm sorry," she said. She realized she'd never learned to say those words, not often enough. "You were right to get me that apartment and I was stupid to have refused your help."

"Well, I wouldn't say stupid. Maybe stubborn." He was grinning, and the joy in his smile took her breath away.

The next words were ones she had never spoken to a man, and she was prepared to fight back her fear. But when she opened her mouth, all she felt was how perfect the moment was, even as they stood in the gymnasium of the Downtown Denver Mission. The sounds of the kids in the gym echoed into the space around them and she could smell the spaghetti the cafeteria had served for dinner.

"I love you, Jack. I think I loved you from the moment we met, but I was afraid to even consider the possibility of giving us a chance."

She stepped forward, reaching up to touch his face. She traced the curve of his lips, the deep indentation of one dimple, the length of his jaw. Holding his gaze, she stood on tiptoes and pressed a kiss to his lips. For a moment he stood still, then he wrapped his arms around her, almost lifting her off her feet.

She had never felt so safe and so loved. He whispered in her ear and a shiver went down her spine. "I love you, Sabrina."

She would never get tired of hearing how he loved her. Letting out a sigh of contentment, Sabrina gazed up into Jack's eyes. His expression spoke of a future together, one that shone bright with promise.

She was lost in the feel of his mouth on hers, the warmth of his arms, and she didn't hear the footsteps behind her.

"*Tía,* what are you doing with Coach Jack?" Gabby stood there, eyes wide. Kassey ran up and put a hand to her mouth, giggling.

Sabrina felt her cheeks go hot. "We'll be done here

in a minute, go back to practice," she called. They ran away toward the group of kids at the end of the gym and the sound of their laughter faded. "How embarrassing."

He lowered his head to kiss her again. She leaned into him, letting his strength add to hers, allowing him to support her with his love. "You'll get used to it," he said.

Sabrina laughed into his shirt, letting her perfect joy outshine all the troubles of her past. She never could have guessed that God's plan for her life included becoming homeless and accepting charity. But as she'd learned to let go of her fear, Jack's love had been there, waiting to lead her to something better, like a map to her heart.

* * * * *

Dear Reader,

Thank you for reading *A Home for Her Family,* and I hope you enjoyed the story of opposites falling in love!

Sabrina struggles with accepting help because she's never really had anyone in her life who was reliable. She's determined to do everything herself, whether or not it's the best way. When she meets Jack, she's instantly attracted to the handsome, fun-loving businessman, but is sure he won't be interested in a girl mechanic from the wrong side of town.

Jack has lived most of his life going along with whatever his father wanted. He went to the college his father picked and went to work at the family business. Jack dreams of leaving it all behind and living a life of freedom up on the mountain. When he meets Sabrina, he sees for the first time how narrow his vision really is and how he's dismissed every blessing he's been given. He yearns to have more of a relationship with Sabrina, but he thinks she can't respect a man who's never really worked for a living.

These two young people learn to see each other through God's grace. We all make assumptions about the people around us, but we also have areas where we need to grow and change. Jack and Sabrina grow in God's love while forging new paths toward happiness.

I pray that you also discover God's abiding love for you and that your future is blessed with every perfect gift!

In Him,

Virginia Carmichael

Questions for Discussion

1. When Sabrina first meets Jack at the mission, what is her impression? Was she correct or did she let her prejudice against the wealthy guide her?

2. Jack asks Sabrina how she chose being a mechanic as her profession. Can you see why she felt this was an odd question? Or do you think every person from every economic level gives the same amount of deep thought to their "calling"? The word means different things to both of them. Do you think this is what caused their first misunderstanding?

3. Jack has been coasting by on his family name, dreaming of the moment he can be free to live his own life. Have you ever realized that your happiness wasn't in some other place, at some other job, but rather right in front of you?

4. Becoming a mother to her nieces has made Sabrina older than her years. Have you ever taken on someone else's responsibility because it was the right thing to do?

5. Sabrina desperately wants to be a good mother to the girls, but she's not sure how. Where can someone like Sabrina look for a role model when she comes from a broken and dysfunctional family? Have you ever mentored a young mom or dad?

6. Jack's parents are distant and not very involved in his life. Why do you think Jack has such a firm

grounding in faith and family? What role does Lili, Gavin's grandmother, play in Jack's life? Did you have a grandparent who brought you closer to Jesus?

7. Sabrina stumbles onto a tragic situation and finds herself with no way to escape because the slave-labor boss threatens her nieces. Can you see how many people turn a blind eye to injustice when their families are threatened? What can a person like you or me do against organized injustice?

8. The manager at Sabrina's apartment house is working to rid the place of anybody who doesn't fit the profile of a young professional. Have you ever experienced discrimination the way Sabrina did, either because of age or color or marriage status?

9. Grant is happy to help Jack arrange Sabrina's new apartment, but he's worried that Jack will regret interfering. Working with homeless families, Grant is familiar with all types of people and he understands Sabrina's need to be independent. What does Grant see about Sabrina's attitude that Jack doesn't? Do you think Grant also knows that Sabrina is in love with Jack?

10. When Rosa calls and asks for money, Sabrina helps her out. Why do you think she helps the sister who ran away and left her to care for the girls? How do you think Sabrina's family encouraged her to always fix what is wrong? Do you think Sabrina

being the oldest had anything to do with her willingness to take on responsibility that's not hers?

11. Why do you think Sabrina doesn't tell the judge that Rosa stole the money? Do you think Sabrina still has growing to do, and that Jack might help her realize that she doesn't need to protect Rosa from the consequences of a bad decision? Have you ever helped out someone who should probably have been left to experience the consequences of their actions?

12. Jack's father is at home recovering from a heart attack during the story. Do you think Jack would have been able to discover the slave-labor evidence if his father had been at work?

13. Many times in this story, the characters are placed in bad situations. As they do their best to follow God's will, they find that willingness helps make wonderful things happen. God worked to bring Jack and Sabrina to a place where they could help rescue the laborers and put away the criminals. Have you ever looked back and seen God's hand in the seemingly unrelated steps that helped someone in desperate need?

REQUEST YOUR FREE BOOKS!

2 FREE INSPIRATIONAL NOVELS
PLUS 2
FREE
MYSTERY GIFTS

Love Inspired

"**W**hat do you do besides work, talk and text on your cell phone, Dale Massey? What do you do for fun?" Faith stepped closer.

Simple fun? He couldn't remember. Every activity had a purpose. Entertaining clients, entertaining women, entertaining his next move as heir to Massey International. "I play tennis, remember?"

Faith shook her head. "The way you play doesn't sound fun at all."

"I play to win. Winning is fun."

She stared at him.

He stared back.

The overhead light bathed Faith in its glow, caressing her hair with shine where it wasn't covered by the knitted hat she wore. Dressed in yoga pants and bulky boots, she looked young.

Too young for someone like him.

"How old are you?"

Faith laughed. "Slick guy like you should know that's no question to ask a woman."

Her hesitation hinted that she might be older than he

thought. She'd graduated college, but when? He raised his eyebrow.

"I'm twenty-seven, how old are you?"

"Thirty."

Faith clicked her tongue. "Old enough to know that all work and no play makes Dale a dull boy."

"You think I'm dull?"

She'd be the only woman to think so. His daily schedule made most people's head spin. Yet this slip of a girl made him feel incomplete. Like something was missing.

Her gaze softened. "You don't really want to know what I think."

He stepped toward her. "I do."

She gripped her mittened hands in front of her. Was that to keep from touching him?

They were close enough that one more step would bring them together. Dale slammed his hands in his pockets to keep from touching her. No way would he repeat today's kiss.

"Honestly, you seem a little lost to me."

He searched her eyes. What made her think that? Lost? He knew exactly where he was going. His future was laid out nice and clear in front of him. But that road suddenly looked cold and lonely.

Will city boy Dale Massey find a new kind of home in Jasper Gulch, Montana, with the pretty Faith Shaw?
Find out in
HIS MONTANA HOMECOMING
by Jenna Mindel,
available November 2014 from Love Inspired.

*Texas Ranger Jake Cavanaugh turns to the one woman
who can help him find his kidnapped teenage daughter.
But there's a lot of history between Jake and Ella, as
well as between Ella and the Dead Drop Killer.
Read on for a sneak peek of
DEADLY HOLIDAY REUNION by Lenora Worth,
available November 2014 from Love Inspired® Suspense.*

"No, no, Jake. He's...he's gone. He hasn't killed anyone
in over five years because he's dead. The trail ran cold
after you found me. You know he was wounded and...he
had to have died in those woods, possibly drowned in the
lake. You were there the night—"

"I was there the night I found you half-dead and just
about out of your mind," Jake said. "But we never found
a body, Ella." He shook his head. "We assumed he was
dead but we never actually had proof."

His eyes held accusation as well as torment. He'd
never forgiven her for following her dream, but he'd sure
brought home the point he'd tried to make when they
broke up way back.

Jake got up and came to her. Putting his hands on her
arms, he stared down at her. "He's back. And he took my
daughter."

Ella refused to believe that. "How do you know it's
him?"

"He left me a note that led me to this."

Ella gasped, her gaze slipping over the necklace, a

delicate gold chain with a white daisy hanging from it. The chain Jake had given Ella for graduation their senior year of high school.

The chain she'd been wearing when the case they'd been working on together had gone bad and the Dead Drop Killer had taken Ella with the intent to kill her in the same way he'd killed four other young women. But she'd escaped because she had been trained to survive. Special Agent Ella Terrell.

He hadn't killed her, but she certainly hadn't been able to do her job anymore. And now Jake was asking her to step back into that world....

She slammed a fist against her old jeans, logic slamming against fear inside her head.

"I came to you because you're the only one who can help me find him." Jake pushed at the bangs falling over Ella's forehead. "I'm sorry, but I need you, Ella."

His touch was as gentle against her skin as a butterfly's fluttering wings. But the look in his eyes was anything but gentle. "And this time, when I do find him, I'm going to end it."

Don't miss
DEADLY HOLIDAY REUNION
by Lenora Worth,
available November 2014 from
Love Inspired® Suspense.

LISEXP1014